I0824449

ALSO BY TOM PERROTTA

Tracy Flick Can't Win

Mrs. Fletcher

Nine Inches: Stories

The Leftovers

The Abstinence Teacher

Little Children

Joe College

Election

The Wishbones

Bad Haircut: Stories of the Seventies

GHOST TOWN

– A NOVEL –

TOM PERROTTA

SCRIBNER

New York Amsterdam/Antwerp London

Toronto Sydney/Melbourne New Delhi

Scribner
An Imprint of Simon & Schuster, LLC
1230 Avenue of the Americas
New York, NY 10020

First Scribner hardcover edition April 2026

Interior design by Jaime Putorti

Manufactured in the United States of America

3 5 7 9 10 8 6 4 2

Library of Congress Cataloging-in-Publication Data has been applied for.

ISBN 978-1-6680-8063-4
ISBN 978-1-6680-8065-8 (ebook)

That ghost is just a kid in a sheet.

—Phoebe Bridgers and Conor Oberst,
"Dylan Thomas"

In memory of my mom, Sue Perrotta

GHOST TOWN

I got an email from the mayor of Creamwood, New Jersey, a woman by the name of Jennifer Rodriguez-Manzoni, inviting me to a ribbon-cutting ceremony for the new municipal building—a combined firehouse, police station, and town hall—which, she was delighted to inform me, had been named the Frank J. Perrini Memorial Complex in honor of my late father.

"We can only imagine how busy you are," she wrote, "but we would be honored if you could join us to celebrate the grand opening of our gorgeous new complex and help us pay tribute to your dad, whose stellar reputation lives on in the memory of our residents, especially the senior citizens, many of whom still remember you fondly as 'Jimmy Perrini' and are justifiably proud of all your success in the publishing and cinematic arenas."

I winced at the sight of my old name—my Creamwood name—which I hadn't used in half a century. I'd gone by Jamie in high school and James in college, and then by Jay Perry, the professional alias I've been using ever since I published my first short story as a graduate student at the Iowa Writers' Workshop.

"If you do decide to join us," Mayor Rodriguez-Manzoni added, "perhaps we can also coax you into giving a reading and book signing at the Creamwood Public Library. After all, you're the only famous writer our town has ever produced! I'm sure we'd get a capacity crowd of all ages for the acclaimed author of *Ghost Teacher* and *Ghost Teacher Loves You* and *Ghost Teacher to the Rescue!*, not to mention the animated series, which my kids enjoyed in their younger days. The library is operating on a very tight budget, as I'm sure you can imagine, so we sadly can't offer anything in the way of an honorarium or travel expenses, but we will wine and dine you at one of the many new restaurants in town. I do hope you'll join us for the opening ceremony. It will be a red-letter day for Creamwood, and a fitting tribute to your father, to whom this town owes a debt that can never be repaid."

I didn't reply to the message, but I didn't delete it, either. I just kept rereading it, surprised by the way it nagged at me, and how much it still hurt to think about that time in my life, the pain encoded in those two simple words:

Jimmy . . . Creamwood . . .

I'd left that place a long time ago and I'd never gone back. I mean, I may have driven through it once or twice in the years when I was still living in New Jersey—it's a hard town to avoid—but I never stopped, never got out of the car, never let my foot touch the ground. I'd drawn a circle around my hometown—cordoned it off from the rest of my life—and that had served me pretty well for a very long time.

Or who knows, maybe it hadn't. Maybe all that stuff catches up to you in the end, the demons you think you've outrun, the bad memories you locked away in a metal box, and then you hid the box in a dark corner of the basement under a heap of dirty blankets, and then you moved far away and did your best to pretend you were someone else. But that box is always right there, right where you left it.

EAT A PEACH

- 1 -

If anyone asked him about his childhood—that broken-off fragment of his life story, a free-floating chapter that felt increasingly strange and distant with the passing years, as if it had happened not just in another time, but to another person in another world—he always gave the same answer.

For a while there, he would say, *we were a normal family.*

There were four of them—Mom, Dad, Denise, and Jimmy. Did they know how normal they were? You bet they did. They didn't brag about it—that would have been weird and the Perrinis weren't weird yet, though that was coming soon enough—but they knew it in their bones, and it gave them a quiet sense of confidence as they moved through their days.

Normal families were the glue that held the world together. Everybody believed that back then; it was like an axiom in math class, a truth so fundamental it didn't need to be spoken out loud, let alone debated. The normal family people got to judge the others, to condemn some of them and feel appropriate amounts of pity for the others, the poor souls who were weird through no fault of their own: old

Mrs. Colangelo, who conversed in public with her mangy-looking French poodle; deaf Georgie Jusczka, who was almost forty but still lived with his mother; wild-eyed Larry Brunner, who'd come home from Vietnam with stumps where his legs used to be, and rolled his wheelchair through the streets of town in all kinds of weather, panting and sweaty and furious, as if he were racing against an invisible opponent.

It wasn't all that hard to be normal in Creamwood back then. You just had to look more or less like everyone else and not do or say anything that would mark you as an oddball or a troublemaker. Denise was a Girl Scout and then a cheerleader, fresh-faced and bubbly, but watchful too. She always glanced around after someone told a joke, waiting an extra second to see if it would be okay to laugh. Jimmy's dad was a volunteer fireman, and a good athlete, despite his comically bulging belly, the kind of guy who played softball with a stubby Dutch Masters cigar jutting from the corner of his mouth. He hit the same single every time he stepped up to the plate, a lazy line drive to shallow center field, and trotted to first base as if he were in no particular hurry to get there. Jimmy's mom was a den mother and a Sunday school teacher and an officer in the PTA. And Jimmy? Well, for most of his childhood, until he was thirteen and everything changed, he was just one of the guys, an easygoing, unobjectionable member of the pack.

You wouldn't have given him a second glance.

At least that was how he remembered it, though he also knew how slippery and unreliable memory could be, how it was always partly a work of fiction, a product of imagination and denial and wishful thinking, and often no better than an outright lie, even when you believed yourself to be telling nothing but the truth.

- 2 -

If you were a stranger passing through in the early 1970s, Creamwood might have struck you as an ugly industrial town—squat brick factories and machine shops lining the railroad tracks, beneath a jagged skyline of smokestacks and rusty water towers. The air would have smelled like bus exhaust, along with an occasional whiff of burning rubber from Danno Plastics, which manufactured the protective mats that went inside urinals, to keep cigarette butts and chewing gum from clogging the pipes.

It was a nicer town once you got off the main drag, tree-lined and residential, street after street of small single-family homes—mostly Cape Cods and split-levels—pressed a little too close together, like soldiers standing at attention. The population density was a source of local pride, five thousand people packed into three-quarters of a square mile. You knew a lot about your neighbors in a place like that, sometimes more than you wanted to.

The houses were alike, and so were the people who lived in them. No one was rich—an above-ground pool or an attached garage seemed like the height of luxury—and it was rare to meet an adult with a college degree, or a father who hadn't served in the military. Almost everyone Jimmy knew was Catholic, and most of them were Italian American. The whole town celebrated the same holidays, ate the same food, watched the same TV shows at the exact same time, and sang along with the same Top 40 on the AM radio.

Oh, and one more thing: they were all white.

Every single one of them.

That might not have been so remarkable if they'd been living in northern Idaho or the cornfields of Nebraska, but Creamwood was just a half hour from Manhattan and only fifteen minutes from Newark, still smoldering from the riots in 1967. Jimmy's dad was a union welder in a sheet metal yard; his neighbors were mail carriers and assembly-line workers and auto mechanics and secretaries. There were probably lots of Black people who did those same kinds of jobs who would have been happy to live in Creamwood, but they weren't welcome. They could work in the gypsum factory or the supermarket or the freeze-drying plant, but they couldn't buy a home or rent an apartment in town. They couldn't even stroll through the quiet streets after dark without being treated to a friendly chat with a police officer.

Later in his life, Jimmy came to understand the history a little better, the combination of racism and white flight and redlining that created segregated suburbs right there in the heart of New Jersey, but he didn't think about it as a kid. Back then, it was just a simple fact of life, part of the natural order.

The sky was blue, the grass was green, and Creamwood was white.

- 3 -

He was thirteen when his mother died. She'd been diagnosed with lung cancer two years earlier and had hung on for as long as she could—longer than anyone expected—fighting against the odds, waiting for a miracle that never arrived.

At least that was how his sister remembered it—a slow, agonizing ordeal, surgeries and hospital stays, their mother wasting away in her bedroom, coughing up blood, the shadow of her illness spreading over everything, darkening the world to the point where it was actually kind of a relief when she passed away.

It wasn't like that for Jimmy, though. He was four years younger than Denise, and his family had gone to great lengths to protect him from the reality of what was happening, and his mother was part of the conspiracy. He had a vivid memory of sitting with her in St. Elizabeth's after her first operation, and somehow finding the courage to ask if she was going to die.

Oh honey, no. She squeezed his hand—the strength of her grip surprised him—and he felt a warm surge of relief spread through his body. *I'm not going anywhere. I'm staying right here with you.*

He had believed her; it was as simple as that. He had banished his fears, or at least buried them deeply enough that he didn't have to stare at them every single day, or imagine a future that might look very different from the past. So yes, Denise was correct: their mother had been sick for a long time and had suffered too much. But Jimmy's version was also true: her death had come out of nowhere, a sucker punch from a bright blue sky.

- 4 -

He was playing baseball on the night she died.

No one had suggested that he might want to stay home that evening, keep her company, say what needed to be said. On the contrary, both of his parents had encouraged him to go to the game, to be a normal kid, to keep on living his life.

So that was what he did—he put on his uniform, wolfed down a pork roll and cheese sandwich, and told his father he was heading to the ballpark.

I'm sorry I can't be there, his father said.

It's okay, Jimmy told him.

His father grunted, like it wasn't okay, but there was nothing anyone could do about it. He made a quick adjustment to the brim of Jimmy's cap and patted him twice on the shoulder. That was about as physical as they ever got with each other.

Good luck, he said. *I'll expect a full report.*

Jimmy hesitated at the door, or at least that was how he preferred to remember it. Maybe he had a premonition. Or maybe he just felt guilty, heading out to play a game while the rest of his family had to stay behind in a house that smelled like Glade air freshener and something else, the thing that the Glade couldn't quite manage to hide.

How's she doing? Jimmy asked.

Okay, his father said. *It's been a long day.*

That must have been good enough for Jimmy, because he left without saying goodbye, and missed his chance forever.

- 5 -

In his defense, it wasn't just any baseball game. It was the Little League Championship Final, the Creamwood equivalent of the World Series. Jimmy played shortstop for Mosquito Control, a team of scrappy underdogs that was hoping for an upset against the heavily favored Knights of Columbus.

Even during warm-ups there was a buzz in the air, a sense that something momentous was about to take place at Carmine J. DeFazio Memorial Park. The bleachers were packed, and the spectators who couldn't find a seat were standing along the bunting-draped chain-link fence that circled the field. It was a heady feeling, being watched by that many people, and Jimmy threw the ball to first base a little harder than usual, as if the game had already started.

When he wasn't fielding practice grounders from Coach McMahon, he kept sneaking glances at the top row of the third-base bleachers, where Janie Randowski was sitting with her friends. She was wearing a light-blue peasant blouse with squiggly red embroidery across the chest, the same shirt she'd worn to the school dance a couple of weeks ago. Jimmy had clutched a fistful of its coarse fabric while they slow danced to "Surfer Girl," the clean scent of lemon shampoo wafting up from her hair, which seemed impossibly dark and glossy when viewed up close like that.

She'd asked him to walk her home, a fifteen-minute journey that they completed in near-total silence, because it was the first time they'd ever been alone together and Jimmy had no idea what to say. She didn't seem to mind, though. Their cautious good night kiss had somehow turned into a full-on make-out session in the driveway, Janie leaning back against the passenger door of her family's Buick Regal, one hand jammed into the back pocket of Jimmy's Wranglers.

It had felt like a thrilling breakthrough at the time, the beginning of something wonderful, but it hadn't turned out that way. She'd been cool to him in school the following Monday morning, and had been avoiding him ever since. She wasn't being mean or anything. She smiled and mumbled a polite hello when they crossed paths in the hallway, but always in a vaguely puzzled way, like she couldn't quite remember who he was, and had no idea why he looked so upset.

But now here she was, sitting on his team's side of the field, wearing that shirt again, and she seemed happy to see him. When he waved to her, she waved back, and when she cupped her hands around her mouth and shouted, *Go Mosquitoes!* in her best cheerleader voice, Jimmy felt a deep sense of relief, like a weight he hadn't known he was carrying had been lifted from his shoulders.

- 6 -

The game was tied 2–2 in the bottom of the third when Greg Cellucci—Mosquito Control's pitcher and Jimmy's best friend—suddenly lost control. He hit the first batter in the leg and walked the next two, loading the bases with no outs. Jimmy felt a leaden sense of dread as Pat Horak, the Knights' best hitter, stepped up to the plate. Pat was as big as a grown man, an adolescent bruiser with a fuzzy charcoal mustache and a belligerent smirk on his face.

Come on, Greggy. Jimmy pounded his fist into his glove. *Just throw a strike. He's no batter.*

Greg took a moment to compose himself, and then he started into his windup, arcing his hands together over his head and lowering them slowly to his chest. He raised his front leg and reared back to throw, and that was when everything fell apart. Pat jumped out of the batter's box and the home plate umpire straightened up, windmilling his arms to signal for a time-out. Greg was too far into his motion to stop; the ball just sort of popped out of his hand and dribbled toward home plate, and by the time it stopped moving, Coach

McMahon was out of the dugout and for some reason he was staring right at Jimmy.

Son, he said, and his voice cracked a little, almost like he was about to cry. *Could you come over here for a second?*

Jimmy didn't understand what was happening until he saw his hippie cousin Wayne slouching by the backstop, an alien presence in white bell-bottoms and a buckskin jacket. He looked scruffy and a little dazed—he just kept shaking his head, as if *no* was the answer to every question in the universe—and all at once, it seemed to Jimmy that everyone in the ballpark was whispering the same word, telling one another that she was *dead*, that she'd been sick for a long time and now she was *dead*, his mother was *dead*, she was *dead*, and then he walked off the field and Wayne made it official, though he didn't actually say the word.

I'm sorry, cuz, he whispered. *I am so fucking sorry.*

- 7 -

His cousin took him home.

It made perfect sense in retrospect—one family member helping another in a moment of crisis—but it hadn't felt that way at the time, because Wayne had been a virtual stranger in the spring of 1974, and the last person Jimmy would have expected to see at one of his Little League games.

In fact, Jimmy had met his cousin only a few months earlier, when Wayne and his new wife, Nilda, had moved into the house next door—a little gray Cape with a dormered attic and a red front door—which had once belonged to Jimmy's grandparents, and was now the property of Wayne's father, Jimmy's Uncle Al.

Jimmy's dad and his older brother were *estranged*—that was the word everyone used to describe the situation—so Jimmy's family was just as blindsided as everyone else on Morgan Street to learn that the Felices, a friendly and popular older couple, would be moving out, and a pair of newlywed hippies would be moving in. The Felices claimed to be leaving of their own free will, relocating to Pennsylvania to be closer to their grandkids, but Jimmy's father said that was bullshit.

Your uncle evicted them, he said. *Al's a cold-hearted son of a bitch. He'd sell his own mother if the price was right.*

Uncle Al was the founder and owner of Perrini Sand & Gravel, a formerly small business that had become a major supplier of road salt to city and county governments throughout northern and central New Jersey. Jimmy's father had no doubt that Al had made some shady deals with some dirty people to get where he was and had tarnished the family name in the process.

Crime doesn't pay, he liked to say. *Unless you're my brother.*

Jimmy's father wasn't crazy about Wayne, either. He'd been nice enough as a little kid, but something had gone wrong after Al had moved his family from Creamwood to Barrington Heights, a tony enclave on the other side of the Watchung Reservation. Wayne had grown up in a mansion with a built-in pool—it was *heated*, a luxury that seemed like the height of decadence to Jimmy's father—and attended a snooty prep school that cost a fortune, though all it had taught him was how to be an ungrateful brat. Like a lot of young people in those days, he'd *rebelled*, as Jimmy's father put it, growing his hair long, protesting the war, smoking pot and doing God knows what else. He'd gotten drafted after flunking out of Glassboro State, but had somehow managed to get himself declared 4-F on account of his supposedly flat feet, despite the fact that he appeared to be in excellent physical condition. And now he was back in Creamwood, attending some classes at community college, freeloading in a house his immigrant grandparents had purchased with a lifetime of sweat and toil.

He's got a tough schedule, Jimmy's father reported. *Basket Weaving on Tuesday, Flag Burning every other Thursday.*

Nilda was a different kind of problem, the subject of gossip and speculation rather than outright disapproval. She was pretty, everyone agreed on that—she had an olive complexion and a cloud of ringlety corkscrew hair that bounced up and down when she walked—but no one knew what she *was.* Her name sounded Spanish, which led some of Jimmy's neighbors to believe that she was Puerto Rican—not completely unheard of in Creamwood in those days, but very rare—though others suggested she could just as easily have been Brazilian or Mexican or even Egyptian. It might have helped clear things up if she'd had an accent, but she sounded just like everyone else.

There was no hostility between the two Perrini households on Morgan Street, but there hadn't been a lot of warmth, either. Jimmy had never shared a meal with his cousin, or had a conversation beyond *Hey, how ya doing?* and now Wayne was hugging him in front of the whole town, whispering words of condolence, because Jimmy's father had sent him there, because there were certain life-and-death errands that could only be entrusted to your own flesh and blood, and this was one of them.

- 8 -

Everyone clapped when Jimmy left the field, the same way they always clapped after a player got hurt. He knew they meant it as a show of kindness and respect, but it still felt weird, almost like they were applauding his mother's death. Some girls in the bleachers yelled, *We love you, Jimmy!* and he was pretty sure one of them was Janie, though he didn't turn around and look.

Wayne kept his arm around Jimmy's shoulders as they walked past the concession stand on their way to the parking area, and Jimmy was secretly glad his cousin had come for him instead of his father or sister. Being with Wayne made him feel older and cooler than usual, and then he felt ashamed of himself for thinking about something so selfish and trivial at a time like that. The girls yelled again that they loved him, and this time Janie's voice was louder and clearer in the mix.

Sounds like you got some fans, Wayne observed.

One of them's my girlfriend, Jimmy said. *At least I thought she was. I'm not really sure anymore.*

Wayne grunted, like he'd been in the exact same situation once or twice, but he didn't elaborate, because they'd already arrived at his car, a beige VW Bug with a green daisy decal on the hood. It was parked illegally in the fire lane, the driver's door flung wide open. Wayne guided Jimmy to the passenger side.

I'm gonna take you back to my house, he said. *Just until your dad and sister get back from the hospital.*

The hospital? A shock of hope jolted through Jimmy's body. *You mean, she's still—*

Wayne made a strange guttural sound, like a wad of misery was stuck in his throat.

She went into cardiac arrest, he said. *The ambulance came and they took her to the emergency room, but they . . . they couldn't get her heart going again. I'm sorry.*

No, Jimmy said. *That doesn't make sense. She has lung cancer. There's nothing wrong with her heart.*

Wayne glanced at the sky. A passenger jet was flying low overhead, banking into a turn, probably circling back to the airport.

Yeah, Wayne said. *None of it makes any sense.*

He opened the door and Jimmy got into the Bug, which smelled like stale pot smoke and motor oil and some kind of sweet perfume. There was a Band-Aid tin on the passenger seat, along with a packet of Zig-Zag rolling papers and an eight-track tape—*Eat a Peach* by the Allman Brothers—and Wayne said to just throw all that crap into the back. Jimmy tossed the Band-Aids and the papers, but the tape had an eye-catching picture on the cover, a cartoon of an enormous peach resting on a flatbed truck, and he stared at it all the way back to Morgan Street.

He kept his eyes glued to the album cover as they pulled into Wayne's driveway. He didn't want to look at his own house, and he didn't want to get out of the car. Luckily, Wayne wasn't in a big hurry. He let the Bug idle for a while, and then he turned off the engine. He leaned toward Jimmy and touched his finger to the tape.

One of the brothers died in a motorcycle accident, he explained. *Duane Allman, great guitar player. He was hit by a peach truck. Only twenty-four years old. That's why they say eat a peach. It's a way to remember.*

Jimmy nodded, but he wasn't thinking about the peaches or the dead guy. He was thinking about his mother, and hoping that Wayne wouldn't ask how old she was, because Jimmy didn't know. She always just said that it was none of his business, or that a lady never told, or that it was for her to know and him to find out. It was embarrassing, being ignorant of such a basic fact about someone you loved, almost like he didn't know her at all, but the mystery was cleared up two days later, when her obituary appeared in the *Star-Ledger* and he found out that she was forty-one.

GIFT CERTIFICATE

- 1 -

The closed coffin looked like a weird piece of furniture, a gleaming wooden capsule resting on a platform in front of an audience of empty chairs. Mr. Tommasini, the funeral director, glanced at Jimmy's father with a solemn expression and lifted the lid.

For a second or two, Jimmy didn't even know what he was looking at.

That's not her, he thought, but then he looked again and it was, and he wanted to yank the lid back down and fasten the latch, because she was a proud woman, and she would not have wanted to be seen in public like that, flat on her back in a lime-green dress, her hair wispy and stiff like a helmet, and all that caked-on makeup, like a clown face painted on top of her own, which was why he hadn't recognized her at first.

He turned to his father, waiting for him to object, but his father just placed his hand on Mr. Tommasini's shoulder—they'd gone to high school together—and gave it a grateful squeeze.

Thank you, Steve. You did what you could.

Jimmy's gaze shifted to Denise, but the only emotion on her face was pure love. She leaned over and kissed their mother on the forehead.

No more pain, she said. *You can go in peace.*

Then she straightened up, and it felt like it was Jimmy's turn, so he bent down and kissed her on the cheek. She didn't smell right, and her face felt cool and unyielding against his lips, dusty from all the powder.

It's me, he whispered. *It's your son, Jimmy.*

A warm hand cupped the back of his neck.

You don't have to say that, his father assured him. *She knows who you are.*

Jimmy nodded, but only because everything was already so horrible, and he didn't want to make it worse.

- 2 -

The viewing room felt way too big at the beginning of the wake, but it filled up quickly. The mourners waited patiently in single file—the way they waited for the Eucharist on Sunday—and then they stood for a few seconds in front of the open coffin, making the sign of the cross, saying a silent prayer, or whispering a few last words into his mother's ear. When they were done, they moved down the receiving line—it was just Jimmy and his father and his sister—and told them what a wonderful person she was, how much she'd done for the Girl Scouts and the PTA and the library, and what a shame it was, because she was so young. But she was in heaven now, reunited with her parents and her older brother, Matthew—technically Jimmy's uncle, though he'd died of polio at the age of ten—and she wasn't suffering anymore, and that was a blessing.

She loved you so much, they told him, over and over and over. *She was always so proud of you.*

After a while, it started to feel like a dream—the smell of flowers, the muffled sobbing, the random faces drifting past. His third-grade teacher. Some guy his father used to bowl with. His Great-Aunt Tillie, whose mouth was twisted by Bell's palsy. The mayor of Creamwood. A barber who'd given him a crew cut when he'd asked for a trim. His Uncle Al and Aunt Gina came too, but they paid their respects quickly and didn't stick around.

A lot of people came in groups. The men from the volunteer fire department wore their dress uniforms, as did the women in the Ladies' Auxiliary. There were Brownies and Girl Scouts and Denise's cheerleading friends. Jimmy's entire Little League team showed up, all of them wearing red hats and jerseys with *Mosquito Control* written across the front. They proudly informed him that they'd won the championship—*We did it for you, Jimmy*—and he thanked them, though it meant nothing to him. He didn't even care that much when Janie arrived with some of her friends—a couple of them were weeping melodramatically, mascara running down their cheeks, though he knew they were only doing it for the attention. Janie gave him a quick businesslike hug—nothing like the way she'd clung to him during "Surfer Girl"—and then she handed him a pink envelope with his name written across the front, the *i* dotted with a heart.

Don't open it now, she told him.

It got to be too much after a while, so he slipped away from his post and went downstairs to the men's room. He peed and washed his hands, and then he remembered something his mother had told him a few months back, after he mentioned that he'd dozed off during science class.

Whenever I got sleepy in school, she said, *I would go to the girls' room and splash some cool water on my cheeks. That always woke me up.*

He followed her advice and it worked. The water cleared his head, and made him feel like she was still there—still watching over him—but his sense of relief only lasted a few seconds, because the door opened and Father Paul, the boyish priest from Our Lady, walked in. He took one look at Jimmy's wet face and completely misread the situation.

It's okay to cry, he said, grabbing some paper towels and pressing them into Jimmy's hand. *There's no shame in that.*

Jimmy dried his face and tossed the towels in the trash. It was awkward to find himself alone in a confined space with Father Paul. The last time they'd spoken was in the confessional, where, after some gentle but persistent prodding, Jimmy had reluctantly admitted to touching himself on certain very rare occasions in a way that he knew was wrong. Father Paul had told him to stop doing that, because it was an offense against God and his own body, but Jimmy hadn't stopped, and he wasn't eager to revisit the subject in the basement of the funeral home. Luckily, Father Paul's mind was elsewhere.

You know, he said, *when something like this happens, it's tempting to blame the Lord, but we shouldn't do that. It's not fair.*

Okay, Jimmy said, even though he did blame the Lord. It was impossible not to.

Father Paul gave him an uneasy look. He was new at Our Lady, and much more popular than Monsignor Blevins, who was grumpy and hard of hearing and burped a lot during mass.

I know it's hard, he said, *but if God chooses to do something like this, we have to believe he does it for a good reason, even if that reason isn't immediately clear. It's our duty to be patient and wait for God to reveal his purpose. Does that make sense?*

I guess so, Jimmy said.

Father Paul frowned and touched the bald spot at the crown of his head. He was still in his twenties, too young to be losing his hair.

Don't turn your back on the church, Jimmy. Will you promise me that?

Jimmy nodded, a bit grudgingly, and Father Paul nodded back, like they'd reached some sort of agreement.

Bless you, my son, he said, and then he drifted over to the urinal.

When Jimmy got back upstairs, he stopped in the entryway of the viewing room. He looked at the body in the coffin—the helmet hairdo, the lime-green dress, the painted-on face—and he heard his mother's voice, as clearly as if she'd been standing at his side.

That's not me, she said.

Something unclenched in his chest. Of course it wasn't her. He'd known it the moment Mr. Tommasini opened the lid.

You don't need to be here, she told him.

He glanced at his father and sister. There was a brief lull in the stream of mourners, and they were both staring straight ahead at nothing, their faces slack and exhausted.

Get some fresh air, his mother told him. *You'll feel so much better.*

- 3 -

She was right about the fresh air, just like she'd been right about the cool water. The sun had gone down and the breeze felt like a feather on Jimmy's face as he slipped out the front door and hurried down the steps to the sidewalk.

Then he stopped, because he needed to get his bearings. The funeral home was an elegant building, red brick with white pillars framing the entrance, but it was located on the corner of Grand and Gleason, in a shabby commercial neighborhood on the edge of town, out near the Parkway entrance ramp. Ike's Rare Coin & Stamp and the Creamwood Trophy Center were right across the street, both closed up for the night, but the Bubble Brite Laundromat was still open, lit up like an aquarium. A single customer sat inside, a middle-aged woman paging through a magazine while her clothes tumbled around in the dryer. Jimmy shut his eyes and concentrated, waiting for his mother's next piece of advice, but there was a deathly silence inside his head, and he started to wonder if maybe he'd only imagined her voice in the funeral home, just to give himself an excuse to get out of there.

He opened his eyes at the exact same moment a car pulled up at the curb in front of him, a powder-blue Chevy Vega with a thick black racing stripe on the hood. The driver was a kid named Eddie Fitzpatrick, who'd only been living in town for a couple of years. He was a grade below Denise, a stringy-haired burnout famous for his arm strength. He didn't play sports, but it was a well-known fact that he could do more pull-ups than anyone at Creamwood High, the gym teachers included. He leaned past the gearshift and peered at Jimmy through the open passenger window.

Need a ride? he asked.

- 4 -

Later in his life, whenever Jimmy thought about that summer, he wondered if anything would have been different if he hadn't gotten into Eddie's car outside the funeral home, if he'd just said, *No thanks*, and continued on his way. It was a moot question, though, because, at the time, it had never even occurred to him that there was a choice to make. He needed to do *something*, and the Vega was right in front of him, so he opened the passenger door and slid inside, and Eddie peeled away from the curb like a bank robber making a getaway.

His father would've been furious if he'd seen it. He'd warned Jimmy a bunch of times to stay out of older kids' cars, because teenage drivers were inexperienced and irresponsible and believed they were immortal.

One stupid mistake, he liked to say. *They'll find out how immortal they are.*

Jimmy didn't care, though. Sitting in the Vega was a lot better than standing next to an open coffin.

Don't blame the Lord. That wouldn't be fair.

He yanked off his clip-on tie and stuffed it into the pocket of his sports coat, but he still felt overdressed compared to Eddie, who was wearing jeans and a flannel shirt with the sleeves torn off, revealing the startling egg-like bulges of his biceps. He reached for the joint smoldering in the dashboard ashtray, took a hit, and offered it to Jimmy.

No thanks, Jimmy said. *I don't . . .*

Pure Colombian gold, Eddie gasped, in a strangled pothead voice straight out of a Cheech and Chong record. *Don't waste your money on shitty Mexican dirtweed.*

He turned the radio up, and they listened to "Truckin'" and "Highway Star" and an endless Bob Dylan song as they cruised up and down the familiar streets. Eddie's eyes kept darting from one side of the road to the other, like he was searching for something in the shadows.

When did you get your license? Jimmy asked, just to make conversation.

Don't have it yet, Eddie said. *My birthday's in September.*

Denise was still on her learner's permit—she'd failed her first two road tests—so Jimmy was familiar with the rules and regulations.

Isn't there supposed to be an adult in the car at all times?

Fuck that. I know what I'm doing.

Jimmy didn't doubt it. Aside from a bad habit of rolling through stop signs, Eddie seemed relaxed and confident behind the wheel, nothing like Denise, who slammed on the brakes for no reason and kept forgetting which turn signal was which.

It's a pretty nice car, Jimmy observed.

Used to be my uncle's, Eddie said. *This thing can fly.*

Can it go a hundred?

Eddie laughed, like that was a stupid question.

Any piece of shit can go a hundred. I'll take you on the Parkway sometime, three or four in the morning when the cops are napping. I'll show you how fast it goes.

Cool, Jimmy said, though he knew it would never happen.

They turned down Alder Road and spotted a group of kids heading toward the schoolyard. It was dark by then, but Jimmy could tell from far away that it was Janie and Greg and some of his other friends. They were eating ice cream cones, and you wouldn't have known from the excited sound of their voices that they'd just come from a funeral home.

Look at that, Eddie muttered. *Little Janie's growing up.*

He slowed the car to a crawl so he could get a better look. Jimmy slumped down in the passenger seat, shielding his face with his hand, because he was suddenly ashamed of himself, riding around with a burnout when he was supposed to be at his mother's wake. He waited a while before sitting back up.

You know what? he said. *I should probably go home.*

Eddie shrugged, like it was all the same to him. He drove to Morgan Steet and pulled up in front of Jimmy's house without having to ask which one it was. Jimmy thanked him for the ride and climbed out. The car was already moving when he shut the door, the rear tires kicking up grit as it roared away.

- 5 -

He didn't have the courage to go inside by himself, so he sat on the front stoop and waited for his father and sister to get home. His Uncle Al's Cadillac was parked out in front of Wayne and Nilda's house, and Jimmy could hear voices coming through the open windows. Uncle Al's was loud and gruff; he did most of the talking and the bulk of the laughing too.

Jimmy felt bad about sneaking out of the wake—he knew he'd let his family down—but it was a muted kind of guilt, nowhere near as bad as what he would have felt if his mother had been alive and he'd done something to disappoint her. She'd always been the disciplinarian in the family, the one who made and enforced the rules, and expected him to be the best version of himself. It was odd to be released from her high standards, to suddenly have so much more room for error.

He'd been waiting there for what had begun to feel like a long time when Uncle Al and Aunt Gina left Wayne and Nilda's house and headed out to the Cadillac. Al was taller and more distinguished than Jimmy's father, the kind of guy who looked like he was born in a suit and tie. Gina was skinny and high-strung, lighting a cigarette as she tottered down the front walk in her high heels. The dome light came on when they opened the doors, and Jimmy caught a quick glimpse of their unsmiling faces before they drove away.

It was almost like they'd timed their departure. The Caddy was barely out of sight when his father's Malibu station wagon turned onto Morgan Street and eased into the driveway. Jimmy raised his hand in a sheepish wave as his father and sister got out of the car. Denise was so mad she wouldn't even look at him.

Asshole, she whispered, brushing past him on her way up the steps.

She went inside, but his father gave him a probing look and sat down next to him on the stoop. He wasn't as upset as Jimmy thought he'd be.

You had us a little worried, he said. *We didn't know where you went.*

I'm sorry, Jimmy told him. *I couldn't breathe in there.*

His father grunted softly, like he knew the feeling.

I wanted to sneak out too, he said, *but I didn't think I could get away with it.*

- 6 -

His mother was everywhere in his bedroom. Not just the collage of family photos that Denise had given him for Christmas, or the orange-and-brown coverlet at the foot of his bed, which his mom had crocheted for him while recovering from her first operation. She was there in the arrangement of the objects on top of his dresser—the bowling trophy, and the coin-sorting machine, and the collection of tiny seashells that she'd brought home from a Cub Scout trip to Sandy Hook—and even in the autographed picture of Bobby Murcer, the Yankees star center fielder, that Jimmy kept in a frame on his desk. She was the one who'd encouraged him to write a fan letter, and coached him on the wording, making sure he requested a signed eight-by-ten photo, if that was at all possible, and it turned out it was.

She was there in the new wallpaper too, pale green with a rustic pattern of pine trees and log cabins and bonfires. She'd selected it the previous summer without any input from Jimmy, though that hadn't been her preference. She'd wanted it to be a *project* for the two of them—*Come on*, she'd said, *it'll be fun*—but he couldn't stand going to furniture stores and paging through binders of wallpaper samples, and he complained so much that she finally gave up and told him he could stay home, and now he felt guilty every time he looked at the walls, because he would have done everything differently if he'd known that was the last summer they'd ever have.

I'm sorry, he told her in his mind. *I should've gone to the store with you.*

He'd forgotten all about Janie's card until he found it in the pocket of his sports coat. It had a picture of a kitten on the front, along with the words *Life Is a Ball of Yarn.* Inside there was a ten-dollar gift certificate to Burger King, along with a brief handwritten message.

I'm sorry about your mom!

It was signed, *Jane Marie Randowski*, which seemed a little formal, though he wasn't completely sure about that, because he'd never received a condolence card before.

He propped it on his desk, right next to Bobby Murcer's smiling face, and then he turned out the light and got into bed. There would be a funeral in the morning and the rest of his life after that. He closed his eyes and waited for his mother to say something, but all he heard were leaves rustling outside his window and a dog barking in the distance. It was a frantic sound, like the dog was trying to get someone's attention, and it went on for a long time. And then it stopped, and the silence that replaced it felt infinite, as cold and empty as outer space.

PART OR PARTICLE

- 1 -

Jimmy missed a week of school after his mother died. It felt like an endless bad dream, the hearse and the hole in the ground, the mass cards and all those bouquets with the shiny banners—*Rest in Peace*, *Our Deepest Sympathy.* Too much sitting around the house, too many neighbors delivering baked ziti in foil-covered pans and cookies in metal tins, too many pastel Kleenexes dabbing weepy eyes, and honking nose blows afterward. Father Paul dropping by at odd hours to see how everyone was doing, maybe say a little prayer for his mother's soul if anyone was up for that. When it wasn't sad it was creepy, and when it wasn't creepy it was boring, and he was glad to finally get back to his old routine.

At least that was what he thought until he actually arrived at school on Monday morning, and felt everyone staring at him like they didn't know him anymore and weren't sure if they were allowed to talk to him. Or even worse, like they were a little scared, like they needed to keep their distance in case he was contagious. He broke into a sweat and his heart started pounding, and he had to duck into the bathroom to splash some cool water on his cheeks, and hide out in one of the toilet stalls until his breathing got back to normal.

When he finally made it to homeroom, he had a fake smile plastered on his face, like everything was just great. Janie gave him a shy little wave as he entered, and Greg did a soft drumroll on the top of his desk. Mr. Kazmierski looked up from his attendance book and gave a brisk nod as Jimmy took his usual seat in the third row.

Good morning, he said, in a weirdly casual voice, as if Jimmy had been out with a cold. *We missed you last week.*

My mother died, Jimmy said. *That's why I was absent.*

It was a dumb thing to say, because everyone knew why he'd been absent—Mr. Kazmierski had attended the wake, along with many of the students in the room—but Jimmy's embarrassment was cut short by a blast of static from the intercom, followed by Principal Cuozzo's gravelly voice, telling everyone to please rise and salute the flag of the United States of America.

- 2 -

Jimmy's heart wasn't in it, but he stood up along with the rest of the class, put his hand on his chest, and recited the words in a clear and forthright manner. He didn't have a choice. Mr. Kazmierski was a stickler for the pledge, and wouldn't hesitate to hand out a detention if he caught you mouthing the words or using a sarcastic tone of voice. Denise said he'd once sent Cheryl Porcaro to the principal's office just for wearing a T-shirt with a peace sign on it.

Patriotism was Kaz's thing, his defining quirk; every teacher had one. Mrs. Carbonetti made her math classes rub their bellies and pat their heads at the same time if she thought they looked sluggish, and Miss Epstein forced them to memorize terrible old poems and recite them out loud.

Hail to thee, blithe Spirit! Bird thou never wert . . .

Kaz had grown up in Creamwood—his parents still lived on Sycamore, over by the park—and everyone knew that his older brother had died in the Korean War, and that was why he was such a hard-ass about respecting the flag and supporting the troops in Vietnam. He had no patience for the protesters, especially the draft dodgers and so-called conscientious objectors, who were just a bunch of hypocrites and cowards who wanted to enjoy the fruits of freedom without making the sacrifices necessary to ensure its survival. He made a big speech about it on Veterans Day, and got so worked up he actually started to cry in front of the whole class.

I'm sorry, he said, once he got a hold of himself. *It just makes my blood boil. My brother gave everything to this country, and he deserves a little respect.*

People were startled by his anger, because, aside from the flag thing, Kaz was one of the more easygoing and approachable teachers in the school. He had shaggy hair, muttonchop sideburns, and a good sense of humor. Chaperoning at a recent fifties dance, he'd dressed up like a Sha Na Na greaser, complete with motorcycle jacket, cuffed jeans, and an unlit cigarette dangling from the corner of his mouth. He did the twist with Miss Argento, and everyone was surprised by how cool they looked.

It was that version of Kaz, the warm and friendly one, who asked Jimmy to stick around after the bell rang. There was nothing but kindness on his face when Jimmy approached the big metal desk at the front of the room.

Son, he said. *It's good to have you back.*

He said he'd been thinking about Jimmy and praying for him and his family. He said he knew what it was like, losing someone you loved at a young age.

It can get lonely, he said, *and your mind can go to some dark places. Do you understand what I'm saying?*

I think so, Jimmy said.

Kaz picked up a pen and scrawled something on a piece of notepaper.

This is my phone number, he said. *If you're ever feeling down, or need someone to talk to, you can call me anytime. I mean it.*

Thank you, Jimmy said, though he couldn't imagine picking up the phone and calling one of his teachers, not even Kaz. It just wasn't in the realm of possibility. He folded the paper with care, tucked it into his back pocket, and started toward the door.

Hold on, Kaz said. *There's one more thing . . .*

Jimmy turned and saw that Kaz's expression had changed. He looked troubled, like there was something difficult he needed to discuss.

I saw your cousin at the funeral home, he said. *With the long hair and the beard? He's your next-door neighbor?*

Jimmy nodded. Kaz wrinkled his nose, like something didn't smell right.

Just be careful, he said. *That's not the kind of role model you need right now.*

- 3 -

Jimmy's father went back to work that same week, and immediately started volunteering for overtime. He'd come home around seven or eight in the evening, sweaty and rumpled, with burn marks on his clothes where the sparks from his welding torch had landed. He'd grab a beer from the fridge, and wolf down a plate of whatever Denise or Jimmy had made for supper. If they asked about his day, he'd just mutter *fine* or *long* or *busy* in a tone that made it clear that that was all he had to say on the subject. He didn't ask how their days had gone.

He was restless after that, full of nervous energy. Instead of settling down in front of a ball game, the way he used to, he started heading outside, mowing the lawn in the twilight or washing the car. One night he even broke out his extension ladder and spent a couple of hours cleaning the gutters in the dark.

When he ran out of yard work, he decided to refinish the kitchen cabinets. It was something Jimmy's mother had wanted him to do for a long time, and it must have felt like a way to honor her memory. He took all the doors off their hinges and brought them down to the basement. For a few days, Jimmy and Denise were driven crazy by the sound of his electric sander. It whirred like a dentist's drill, drowning out whatever they were watching on TV.

He got the doors stripped and prepped, and then he just stopped. He kept going down to the basement, but they never heard any work noise, and the doors never got repainted. That whole weird summer, the kitchen cupboards were wide open, their innards displayed to the world. Anything you wanted, you could just reach in and grab it.

- 4 -

Around that same time, Wayne and Nilda invited them over for supper. They'd become a lot friendlier since the funeral. Whenever Nilda went food shopping, she rang the doorbell and asked if there was anything they needed. If Denise or Jimmy needed a ride somewhere, Wayne said he was happy to take them in the Bug.

You're family, he would say. *We gotta take care of each other.*

It was only Denise and Jimmy who accepted the dinner invitation; their father said he had some kind of meeting at the firehouse, though that was probably just a euphemism for going out to a bar with some of his firemen buddies. Or at least it would turn into one over the course of the summer.

Jimmy knew his sister occasionally drank alcohol at parties, but she was a prude about weed, and frequently complained about all the potheads wandering the halls of Creamwood High. She had to hide her disapproval when Wayne answered the door with a joint in his hand and offered her a toke.

No thank you. Denise smiled stiffly. *It's a little early for me.*

She loosened up a bit once they got settled in the living room, which was surprisingly normal-looking. Jimmy and Denise sat on the brand-new, plaid-patterned couch that Nilda said was a wedding gift from Wayne's parents. It was part of a set, along with a matching love seat and armchair.

Not necessarily our style, she said. She was wearing a pale blue apron over cutoffs and a T-shirt. *But it was very generous of them.*

Wayne made a gun out of his thumb and index finger and brought it to his temple.

It was an offer we couldn't refuse, he said, and then he pulled the trigger.

The art on the walls seemed a little more their style than the furniture. There was a vintage *Casablanca* poster above the couch, and over the love seat, a framed abstract print—a sloppy yellow rectangle levitating over an even sloppier orange one—that Jimmy wasn't sure he liked, but couldn't stop looking at.

Wayne poured some Gallo Chablis for himself and Nilda and Denise, and some iced tea for Jimmy, and they drank a toast to his mother's memory. It was meant as a nice gesture, but it felt wrong somehow, like everyone was having a great time without her, and Jimmy only pretended to drink, while silently apologizing to her in his mind.

It was a little awkward at first, because they didn't know one another that well, but Nilda kept the conversation moving. She quizzed Jimmy about his baseball season, and the sports he wanted to play in high school, and Jimmy could feel himself blushing and looking at his feet as he answered, because the weather had gotten warm over the past week, and Nilda had taken to sunbathing in her backyard in a white bikini. While she was out there one afternoon, just minding her own business, he had spied on her through his bedroom window and done something he wasn't proud of, and the memory made it hard for him to look her in the eye.

When she'd completed her interview with Jimmy, Nilda got Denise talking about her relationship with Nick Filiakis, the guy she'd been dating since freshman year.

Is he cute? she asked.

Yeah, Denise said. *He's got beautiful eyes. Really long lashes.*

Do you have a picture?

As a matter of fact, senior prom photos had just arrived, and Denise fished the envelope out of her purse. She shuffled through the prints until she found the couple portrait, the two of them standing in profile, their faces turned toward the camera. It was a relic from a happier time, just a week before their mother's death.

I'm wearing heels, Denise explained. *That's why he looks so short. Usually we're the same height.*

I love your dress, Nilda said. *I'm not so sure about your boyfriend's tux, though. What color is that?*

I think it's called pewter. And I'm not sure how much longer he's gonna be my boyfriend.

Oh. Did you guys have a fight?

No. It's just . . . Nick's going to college in Delaware in a couple of months, so what's the point?

Well, you still have the summer, Nilda told her. *Doesn't have to be forever, right?*

Denise hesitated, then leaned forward and spoke to Nilda in a confidential voice, as if Wayne and Jimmy weren't even there.

He only wants one thing, you know? I just want to wait a little while.

Jimmy was surprised to hear this, and more relieved than he expected to know that Denise and Nick hadn't gone all the way.

Good for you. Nilda handed the photo back to Denise. *When the right guy comes along, you'll know.*

Denise nodded, grateful for the support.

What about you? she asked. *Did you have a good time at your prom?*

Me? Nilda looked amused. *That wasn't really my scene.*

She dropped out of high school, Wayne explained in a matter-of-fact voice. *Ran away and joined the Hare Krishnas.*

Jimmy thought he was joking, but Nilda gave a good-natured shrug, guilty as charged.

It was only for a couple months, she said. *And there are worse things than chanting in the subway, believe me.*

I rescued her from a cult. Wayne grinned, like it was all good fun. *And she never even thanked me.*

Nilda didn't deny it. She jerked her thumb in Wayne's direction and shook her head.

And now I'm married to this clown and living in Creamwood, New Jersey. I'm not sure that thanks are in order.

- 5 -

Denise graduated in early June, less than a month after their mother's death. Decades later, Jimmy could still remember how raw and exposed he'd felt, walking with his father from the parking lot to the football field. They were a little late and had to weave their way through the early birds, nodding and whispering apologies as they made their way up to the top row of the bleachers.

It was a warm and unpleasantly humid evening, the sky streaked with pink over the flat roof of the high school. Some of Jimmy's friends were sitting in a group a few rows down, Greg and Janie among them—they both had siblings in the graduating class—and they turned around and beckoned him to join them.

Go ahead, his father said. *Don't mind me.*

It's okay, Jimmy told him. *I'm fine right here.*

His father squeezed his knee, and Jimmy felt good about that. He hoped it would make up, at least a little, for the way he'd abandoned his family at the wake.

It was a long ceremony. The glee club sang the national anthem, the principal made a few remarks, and then there were full-length orations from the top two students in the graduating class. The valedictorian was a pale, redheaded girl named Olivia Jean Riley, unusually tall and very thin. She stood at the podium for a long time without speaking, almost like she'd forgotten why she was there. There were a few catcalls, and then she bent toward the microphone, holding her mortarboard in place with one hand.

I become a transparent eyeball, she said, in a soft and dreamy voice. *I am nothing; I see all; the currents of the Universal Being circulate through me; I am part or particle of God.*

Hoo boy, Jimmy's father whispered. *Here we go.*

Afterward, a lot of people complained about the speech—apparently she went on and on about Ralph Waldo Emerson—but Jimmy barely heard a word of it. He was too distracted by Janie and Greg, who had become enmeshed in an intense, whispered conversation. He didn't like how close together they were sitting, and he hated not knowing what they were talking about, because it looked like they were telling each other one amazing secret after another, and maybe even falling in love, though Greg said that was ridiculous when Jimmy questioned him about it in school the following morning.

It was nothing, he insisted. *We were just goofing around.*

- 6 -

There were no speeches at Jimmy's eighth-grade commencement the following week, which was held inside the junior high auditorium. It was sweltering in the big windowless room, all the parents and grandparents and siblings packed together in the narrow seats, checking their watches and fanning themselves with their programs.

He didn't remember much about the ceremony beyond the procession itself, the terrible thing that happened as the graduates marched down the center aisle in their caps and gowns, coming to a full stop after each and every step. He was scanning the crowd as he walked, trying to locate his father and sister, when he caught a flash of lime green at the edge of his vision, and a smile full of love, and an incredible feeling surged through his body—a shock of happiness beyond anything he'd ever known—but then he turned and looked again, and it wasn't his mother, not even close. It was a brutal letdown, the first of many similar false alarms he would suffer in the years to come, a phenomenon that usually occurred when he was alone in a crowd, searching for a familiar face. The rush of misguided joy always came and went in a split second, but the hollow feeling that replaced it could sometimes last for days.

There was a big party that night in Valerie Bruno's backyard. He walked over by himself—he could hear the Doobie Brothers blasting from a block away—and headed up the empty driveway, which Valerie and her friends had decorated with a series of festive messages written in colored chalk: *School's Out!!! Party Time!!! We Are Creamwood!!! Let's Get Rowdy!!!*

He made it all the way up to the gate, and then he stopped and listened to the thumping music and the excited chatter and the raucous laughter on the other side of the tall wooden fence—all those kids he'd known forever having the time of their lives—and he just didn't feel like he was part of that anymore, so he turned around and left, smearing the stupid graffiti with the sole of his sneaker as he made his way back down the driveway.

- 7 -

He was halfway home when the powder-blue Vega rolled up beside him. Jimmy wasn't surprised, even though he hadn't seen it since the night of the wake. He opened the passenger door and got in.

No party? Eddie asked.

Not for me, Jimmy told him.

Eddie nodded, like no further explanation was necessary, and pulled away from the curb. They drove in silence through the residential streets on the south side of town, then turned onto Grand and headed past the factories. The perforating plant had a second shift, and some of the workers were loitering outside on their break, smoking and eating sandwiches and watching the traffic go by.

Oh man, Eddie said. *Look at those poor bastards.*

They stopped at the Quick-Chek to buy two cans of Nehi root beer, the only soda Eddie would drink. He gave one to Jimmy and balanced the other between his legs as they cruised around the north side. He slowed down like a tour guide whenever they passed a house where a good-looking girl lived, or some other piece of neighborhood trivia came into his mind.

You know Mary Beth Martini? She's in the color guard. Always walking around with that fake wooden rifle. That's her bedroom, up in the attic.

Old Man DiLeo goes deep-sea fishing every week. You can smell his garbage cans a mile away in the summer time. I saw one of the garbagemen puke once, after he opened the lid.

Jimmy nodded and sipped his root beer. It was oddly relaxing, driving around and listening to Eddie's commentary. Valerie Bruno's party felt impossibly far away, like it was happening on another planet.

Tina Kubiak's older sister works in a topless bar. She's not a dancer, though. Just a waitress.

As they turned back onto Grand, Eddie produced a wrinkled joint from behind his ear and lit up. He took a big hit to get it going, and then he offered it to Jimmy.

Come on, he said. *Don't leave me hanging.*

Jimmy pinched the joint between his fingers and took an amateurish puff that seared his lungs and triggered a coughing fit that made him double over. Eddie took his hand off the gearshift and thumped him gently on the back until it went away.

It's a little harsh, he said. *But it's really good. I bought it from a buddy of mine who works at McDonald's. He sticks it in the bag with the burgers and fries. All you have to do is ask for extra ketchup. That's the secret code.*

Come on, Jimmy said. *You can't buy weed at McDonald's.*

You can if you know the right people, Eddie told him. *You just gotta be cool about it.*

Jimmy was more careful with the second toke, and only coughed a little. He tried to return the joint, but Eddie waved him off.

Keep it, he said. *It's your graduation present.*

Molly and I were eating dinner on the patio when my sister called. I was surprised to hear from her. We'd fought about politics in 2016—she and her husband had gone full MAGA, right from the start—and now we hardly ever talked except around the holidays or to wish each other a happy birthday. We'd never been that close to begin with, and living on different sides of the country had given us a convenient excuse for keeping it that way.

"Are you coming?" she asked. "To this thing for Dad?"

"I don't think so," I said. "It's a long trip."

She didn't answer right away. I tried to picture her on the other end of the line, a stout gray-haired woman with an artificial hip, but in my mind she was always seventeen, slender and pretty, heading out the door to join her friends, who were waiting out front in a Camaro or Dart, Jackson Browne or Elton John blasting from the open windows.

"Jesus Christ, Jimmy. Can't you do this one little thing for your family?"

"It's not little," I said. "Not for me."

"I get that," she said, in a softer tone. "I grew up in the same house as you, in case you forgot."

I wanted to tell her it was different, because she was older when it all fell apart, basically an adult, and I was just getting started. That was how it had felt to me for a long time—like she was the luckier one—but I didn't believe that anymore. She'd lost just as much as I had, and never had the luxury of starting over. I got to be Jamie and James and Jay, but she was always just Denise.

"Come on, Jimmy." There was a pleading note in her voice I hadn't heard for a long time. "Don't make me do this alone."

Molly was watching me when I put down the phone. She'd been pushing me to stay in better touch with my sister, despite our political differences. Her own siblings were really important to her—she talked or texted with them almost every day—and she didn't think it was healthy for me, having so little contact with the only surviving member of my family, cutting myself off from all of our shared history, and leaving Denise out in the cold.

"What was that all about?" she asked.

"Creamwood," I said. "They're naming a building after my dad."

I found the mayor's email on my phone and showed it to her. She looked puzzled, and a little hurt.

"Why didn't you tell me about this?"

"I don't know," I said. "I'm still trying to wrap my head around it."

A flicker of frustration passed across her face—one of her big complaints over the years was that I kept too much of myself to myself—and then she turned back to the email.

"The Frank J. Perrini Memorial Complex," she said. "Your therapist is gonna have a field day with that."

"No kidding," I said. "I might have to start going twice a week."

She pursed her lips and tilted her head, making a poor-baby face to acknowledge my pain and maybe mock it a little too, because my problems weren't all that serious in the grand scheme of things. I was just struggling a bit, emotionally and professionally, finding it difficult to visualize a happy and productive future for myself. It was a garden-variety case of the midlife blues, nothing that couldn't be cured with a little Zoloft and some pickleball, or so everyone told me.

"On the bright side," she said, "they seem to have gotten the impression that you're a famous writer."

"They're just being polite."

"Don't be so modest," she said. "You've done all right for yourself."

She made a vague but expansive motion with her hand, a gesture meant to encompass our house in the hills, the new kitchen and the infinity pool and the art on the walls and our excellent view of the city twinkling below, all of which had been made possible by *Ghost Teacher*, the animated kids' show I'd created and run for four seasons. It had been a slog from the start and it hadn't gotten any easier with time, the endless hours in the writers' room and the editing bay, all the haggling with executives, the nitpicking notes and lateral-move revisions, followed by different notes from younger executives who'd replaced the old ones, all the stress and stomach upset and mental turmoil it took to produce a show that was mediocre at best, and I sometimes wondered if it had all been worth it.

But that was the past—my Faustian bargain was a fait accompli—and there was no going back. And it wasn't really what Molly was talking about anyway, or not just that. She was also referring to our life together—our marriage, our two beautiful grown-up kids, everything we'd shared since the night we met at a New Year's Eve party in Brooklyn in 1984—and the value of that was something I'd never doubted, not for a moment.

"You're right," I told her. "I've got nothing to complain about."

She nodded briskly, as if that was the correct answer, and then her face turned wistful.

"I wish I'd met your dad," she said. "I think I would've liked him."

BIRDHOUSE

- 1 -

It was Olivia Jean Riley, the high school valedictorian, who introduced him to the Ouija board. It must have been the middle of July when it happened, just a week or two after Jimmy had started helping out at Creamwood Summer Rec, where Olivia was the arts and crafts counselor.

The first time she mentioned it, he thought she'd said *weegee* board, and she had to spell it out for him letter by letter. She explained that *Ouija* was a compound of the French and German words for *yes*, though in her opinion the name gave a misleading impression of what the board was for, and what it was capable of.

It's not a toy like the Magic 8 Ball, she told him. *It doesn't just say Yes or No or Ask Me Later. And it's not gonna tell you if your cute little girlfriend has a new boyfriend or anything like that.*

Jimmy nodded, though he was a little unsettled by the reference to his *cute little girlfriend,* because rumor had it that Janie and Greg had disappeared for a long time in the middle of Valerie Bruno's party and had returned with guilty smiles on their faces. He'd also heard that Greg had visited the Randowskis' beach house in Lavallette over the Fourth of July weekend, and had supposedly slept over on the living room couch.

I don't have a girlfriend, he said.

Olivia nodded in slow motion, like she didn't believe him, but wasn't going to argue the point.

I've got a Ouija board, she said. *If you're interested, I could show you how it works.*

Jimmy was surprised by the offer, because he hadn't yet begun to think of Olivia as a friend. Friends were peers, people you were on an equal footing with, and she was more like a local celebrity, a bigger-than-life individual whose exploits he'd been hearing about for as long as he could remember.

Olivia wasn't just the smartest kid in his sister's class; it went way beyond that. She'd scored higher on the SATs than anyone in the history of Creamwood High, an achievement made even more impressive by the fact that she'd skipped fourth and sixth grades, so she was actually two years younger than the rest of the kids taking the test, and only two years older than Jimmy. According to Denise, Olivia kept a telescope in her bedroom and could identify all the constellations in the night sky. She'd also taught herself to read Braille, and had published an award-winning sonnet in a national magazine for kids, something about a mermaid who couldn't understand why everyone was staring at her at the carnival.

All that should have made her an easy target for mockery, but she didn't get picked on very much, probably because people felt sorry for her. Her family had been in a tragic car accident when she was seven. Her father and baby brother were both killed, and it was just her and her mother after that, and her mother had what Jimmy's parents politely referred to as a *drinking problem.*

There were lots of embarrassing stories about Mrs. Riley—most of them took place at the bar in Creamwood Lanes—but Jimmy had only ever seen her at Stop & Shop, where she worked as a cashier. Her hair was a brassy bouffant, and her blood-red lipstick wasn't always applied with a steady hand. Jimmy's mother used to say that it was a mystery of life, how a woman like that had raised such a brilliant daughter.

- 2 -

He had felt lost at the beginning of school vacation, abandoned by everyone. His father left for work at seven in the morning, and Denise headed off an hour later for her job as a mother's helper in Laurel Grove. By the time Jimmy rolled out of bed, the house was empty and he was on his own.

The silence felt bleak and a little ominous, like something bad was about to happen, even though the bad thing had already come and gone, which was why no one was waiting for him in the kitchen, smiling and calling him a sleepyhead and asking what he wanted for breakfast. There was just the dusty morning sunlight flooding in through the window above the sink, falling onto the oval table with its four empty chairs, one more than they needed.

Sometimes there was a note from his father or Denise tucked beneath the sugar bowl—*Take out garbage . . . Buy milk . . . WHERE IS SPATULA???*—but more often than not the only sign of life was a dirty coffee cup where his father had sat, or a plate with a few crumbs on it.

The first thing he did was turn on the radio, which was where it had always been, on the counter next to the toaster, though it was no longer tuned to WOR, the AM station his mother had loved. He and Denise preferred WPLJ, 95.5 on the FM dial. Jimmy liked most of the songs well enough, but the DJs were even better. They always sounded so upbeat, even after they played something really sad—"Taxi" by Harry Chapin, or "Captain Jack" by Billy Joel—as if nothing could possibly spoil their excellent mood. He thought it might be a job he'd like to do someday—*Hey, it's Jimbo, putting the music in your morning*—but it seemed like an idle dream, not something that could ever happen in real life.

Breakfast was either Cap'n Crunch or Lucky Charms. Jimmy hated milk, so it was just the dry cereal in a bowl. He could have sat anywhere, but he always went to his usual spot, the chair directly facing the sink and the window, even though the glare was sometimes a problem. It was comforting to sit where he was supposed to, right across from the chair where his mother used to sit, and it wasn't that big a deal if he had to squint a little while he ate. When he was finished, he put the dirty bowl and spoon in the dishwasher and went back upstairs for his morning shower, another wholesome and reassuring part of his day.

The not-so-wholesome stuff happened after that, when he headed into his bedroom with a towel wrapped around his waist. He told himself to hurry up and get dressed and get out of there—to resist the temptation to check on Nilda—but it was already too late for that.

She wasn't usually outside—morning wasn't her sunbathing time—but it didn't matter. Just standing by the window, peering down at the section of the yard where she liked to spread out her towel, was enough to get him started. He could picture it so clearly, the way she leaned back on her elbows and tilted her face to the sky, the way she untied her bikini top just before she rolled onto her stomach. She looked amazing like that, face down in the grass, curly hair fanned out around her shoulders, her bare brown back, the bikini bottoms that didn't quite cover her butt cheeks, and just thinking those words—*bikini bottoms, butt cheeks*—jolted him into a higher gear, and it only took a minute or two before it was happening again, the pleasure pumping out of his body and the shame rushing in to take its place.

- 3 -

He couldn't stay home after that—it was too depressing—and couldn't think of anywhere to go except Lenape Park, a complex of athletic fields and woods that formed the southern border of town. It was Creamwood's oasis, a haven for dog walkers and stroller-pushing young mothers and elderly bench sitters and brooding chain-smokers. You could play softball or touch football or tennis at Lenape, or have a cookout with your family on a Sunday afternoon. You could toss a Frisbee on a spring day, or catch some rays, and if you needed a little privacy, you could wander into the woods and do whatever the hell you wanted. In wintertime, kids went sledding on the hill above the parking lot, and in the summer it was the site of a town-sponsored youth recreation program that had been a big part of Jimmy's childhood. They had arts and crafts for the little kids, sports and games for the older ones, and a picnic pavilion everyone could shelter under if it rained.

At thirteen, Jimmy had aged out of Summer Rec—the kids who attended were ten and under—so he made himself useful to the counselors in any way he could, helping to set up the Ping-Pong table and the Nok-Hockey board, and volunteering to umpire chaotic Wiffle ball games played by ornery nine-year-old boys who argued after every play and called each other vile names and regularly threatened to kick each other's asses. He also ran errands for the counselors, riding his bike over to Sturmer's Deli for cartons of iced tea and Hostess Fruit Pies and packs of cigarettes, and in return they let him stick around and eat lunch with them in the picnic pavilion. It was a privilege—he was the only civilian at the table—and he was happy just to be included, to sit quietly and soak up their conversations about Watergate and ancient astronauts and the disgusting things they'd witnessed at the Port Authority Bus Terminal in the city.

It helped that Denise's ex-boyfriend, Nick Filiakis, was the sports counselor. Nick was a great athlete and also a bit of a dick—he'd been voted Best Physique and Biggest Ego by his senior classmates—but he was going out of his way to be nice to Jimmy, because Denise had broken up with him a few days after graduation, and Nick wanted her back. He kept pumping Jimmy for information, asking what his sister was up to and who she was hanging out with, and he seemed a little wounded and pathetic about it, which cut him down to size in a way that Jimmy appreciated.

There were three other counselors on the staff. The top dog was Doug Rizzetti, a clean-cut frat boy who'd just finished his freshman year at Rutgers. College had surpassed his wildest expectations, except that he'd partied a little too hard and flunked out of Organic Chemistry. He wasn't sure if he should try again, or just give up on his childhood dream of becoming a doctor.

Greek life is pretty demanding, he said. *And it's only gonna get worse once I start living in the house. Maybe I should switch to accounting or food science or something.*

Maybe you should just quit your dumb frat, Heather Cataldo suggested. *You know, focus on your studies.*

Sure, Doug said. *And maybe you should quit smoking.*

Heather chuckled and took a deep, squinty-eyed drag on her Marlboro. She was the laziest and least qualified of the counselors—everyone knew she'd only been hired because her father was the mayor's cousin—and she flouted the dress code on a daily basis, wearing tube tops instead of the official Rec Department T-shirt, and presided over the games table with an air of regal indifference, painting her nails and practicing her smoke rings right in front of the little kids, who knew better than to bother her with their petty requests.

And by the way, Doug told her, *frats aren't just about parties. We do a lot of charity work too. Like we have a winter sock drive for disadvantaged children, that sort of thing. 'Cause, you know, a lot of these poor kids, they don't have warm socks or anything.*

Olivia sat a little apart from the rest of the group, reading a novel called *The Magic Mountain* that she'd borrowed from the library. Nobody seemed offended by this; it was just who she was, the straight-A student, the genius with her nose in a book. It was weird, though. Every once in a while, when one of the others said something unusual—like when Doug mentioned the winter sock drive—she would glance up from the page as if someone had whispered her name, and dart her eyes in Jimmy's direction, as if he were the one who'd done the whispering. It happened so fast, it was almost like it hadn't happened at all.

- 4 -

He had only been helping out at Rec for a week or so when Doug interrupted lunch with a strange request.

Hey, Jimmy, he said. *Could you take your shirt off?*

What?

You heard me. Take it off.

Jimmy glanced uncertainly at the other counselors, and they all nodded, even Olivia. They were at their usual table in the pavilion, just the five of them. He didn't want to be a bad sport, so he put his sandwich down, and then he stood up and removed his T-shirt. He was used to being bare-chested in the summer, but it was still a little awkward, displaying his body to the counselors. Nick put two fingers in his mouth and let loose with a wolf whistle.

Nice muscles, Heather told him, and he couldn't tell if she was joking or not.

Olivia didn't say anything, but she was staring at him so intently he could feel it on his skin.

All right, Doug said. *Close your eyes.*

Once again, Jimmy did as he was told, though he was starting to get nervous, like maybe a prank was afoot. There was a moment of stillness—he could hear the insects humming in the trees and the sound of his own breath—and then a flurry of motion, the others pressing in and surrounding him. Someone slipped a collar over his head, and then they were yanking on his arms, threading his hands through sleeves, and tugging everything into place.

Okay, Doug said. *You can look now.*

Jimmy opened his eyes and saw that he was wearing an official Creamwood Recreation T-shirt, the exact same one as everyone else, except for Heather, who was wearing a turquoise tube top.

Is this for real? he asked. The shirt was canary yellow with the word *COUNSELOR* written across the chest in big black letters. *I can keep this?*

Doug nodded and ruffled his hair.

You earned it, brother. Welcome aboard.

Nick gave him a big thumbs-up, Heather blew him a kiss, and Olivia clapped politely, barely making a sound. Jimmy wanted to thank them, but all he could do was smile.

- 5 -

A few days later—it was a drizzly morning in mid-July—Olivia asked for his help with a crafts project in the pavilion. The kids were making birdhouses out of Popsicle sticks, an activity that required patience and fine motor control. There was a lot of Elmer's glue caked on a lot of little fingers, which meant that it was easy for the kids to pick up the sticks, but not so easy to let go of them. Some of the younger ones got pretty frustrated, and a few were close to tears. Jimmy ended up doing a fair amount of the assembly, and quite a bit of decorating as well, sprinkling glitter on the wet paint, and affixing elbow macaroni and tiny ceramic tiles to the walls.

It was absorbing work, and the kids were grateful. The only problem was, he had built a summer rec birdhouse of his own when he was five or six years old, and brought it home to his mother. He'd buried the memory for a long time, but that morning it forced its way back to the surface with distressing clarity, not just the humble gift itself—it was green and yellow, with multicolored buttons adorning the roof—but the look of wonder and delight on his mother's face when she lifted it from his cupped hands.

I love it, she told him, and she planted a big kiss on the top of his head. *If I was a bird, this is where I would live.*

The memory cracked something open inside of him, like he'd somehow forgotten what had happened to her, and now he had to face up to it all over again. He didn't cry in front of the kids. He just got up from the picnic table, left the pavilion, and walked across the wet grass to the hut that contained the restrooms on one side and the equipment shed on the other.

It was dim and cool inside the shed, and he just stood there, thinking about his mother's face and how unfair it was that he would never get to see it again except in photographs, and would never get to hear her laugh, or make that soft *mmm* sound in her throat, the one she made when he told her something interesting or surprising.

Olivia didn't announce herself. She just sort of materialized at his side and kept him company while he stared at the cinder block wall. She was holding a paintbrush in her hand, and after a while she touched the damp bristles to the back of his wrist and told him there was a way to talk to dead people, if that was something he ever wanted to do.

IN THE CREEPMOBILE

- 1 -

Working at Rec gave a structure to his days, kept him busy and sane and connected to the world. He felt important in his yellow shirt—he was a *COUNSELOR*, wise beyond his years, a person the little kids could turn to if they needed help or advice or a bit of friendly encouragement. He was always happy to play some catch or lose a game of checkers or tie someone's shoelace before they tripped and hurt themselves.

It was different at night. At night he was just himself again, barely a teenager, alone and adrift. Later in his life, when he tried to make sense of that summer, his heart went out to the boy he'd been. He couldn't understand what his father and sister had been thinking, how they'd left him to his own devices at a time when he needed them the most. What was strange was how natural it had felt while it was happening, as if everybody was just doing the best they could under some pretty miserable circumstances.

His father usually got home late from work—there was a lot of overtime that summer—ate a quick dinner, and then rushed right out again, supposedly to attend yet another *meeting* at the firehouse.

It was unclear what happened at these gatherings, or where he went afterward, but he usually stayed out pretty late, and was off to work before Jimmy woke up in the morning.

His sister was busy too. She still hadn't passed her driver's test, but one or another of her friends was always sounding the horn out front in the early evening. One of the guys from her crowd, this joker named Dan Sparzino, had a Trans Am whose horn made an *Aah-YOO-Guh* sound, the kind you'd expect from an old jalopy. Everyone thought it was hilarious the first time they heard it.

Before she left the house, Denise always took a moment to brush her hair and check her makeup, and then she'd turn to Jimmy and ask if he had any plans.

Not really. Just hanging out with the guys.

Behave yourself, she would warn him in a not-quite-serious voice, because it wasn't really her job to keep tabs on him. *No smoking or drinking. And try to be home by ten.*

What about you? Jimmy would ask, because he knew Nick would grill him the following morning about what Denise had been up to, and what she'd been wearing when she left the house. *You going on a date or something?*

Maybe, she would say. *Who wants to know?*

Jimmy would shrug and make a mental note of her outfit, though it was rarely anything special, usually just cutoffs or a denim skirt, and some kind of sleeveless summer top.

I'll expect you home by midnight, he would say.

That always made her smile, when he tried to turn the tables like that.

Okay, Dad, she would say, and then she'd grab her purse and leave, and Jimmy would head out a few minutes later, because being alone in the house at night was the only thing worse than being alone in the house in the morning.

- 2 -

Sometimes he went to the Little League to hang out with his old gang, but it wasn't much fun. They were a mixed group of guys and girls, members of the popular crowd, and mostly they just sat in the bleachers and gossiped about who liked who, and the new couples that had formed at one or another of the graduation parties, and Jimmy had nothing to contribute, because he'd missed all the parties, and because the whole subject of couples had become a sore spot for him, a source of pain and embarrassment.

Janie was still away—her family spent the summer at their beach house—but Greg was sometimes around, and those nights were the worst, because what could you say to your former best friend who'd stolen your girlfriend right after your mom died? It didn't matter that Janie hadn't really been his girlfriend, not in any official way. It was more the principle of the thing, Greg knowing how much Jimmy liked her, and stabbing him in the back anyway, and never even trying to apologize.

But it wasn't just Greg. Jimmy was out of sync with all of them. It was like they'd become this tight unit in the past couple of months, bonded by all the fun they'd had in his absence. Sometimes he didn't even know what they were talking about. One of them would say something—just a simple word or phrase—and they'd all start cracking up, like it was the funniest thing they'd ever heard. Jimmy would force himself to join in, because it was even worse to sit there stone-faced, while they all laughed their heads off.

When he couldn't take it anymore, he made up an excuse and started walking in the general direction of home, though he had no intention of actually going there. He was just killing time, wandering up one side street and down another. He liked the hush in the air, and the lit-up houses, and the way his mind would slow down and empty out as he walked, random songs popping into his head out of nowhere—"Ruby Tuesday," "Sugar, Sugar"—and he just kept going until Eddie found him.

It always happened fast, the Vega careening around a corner, screeching to a halt beside him. Jimmy would jump in, Eddie would hit the gas, and the night would start over.

- 3 -

Eddie wasn't very popular with kids his own age. He didn't have a group of guys he hung out with, and a lot of people Jimmy knew made sour faces when his name came up in conversation, because it was kind of a town-wide joke, how desperate Eddie was, always trying to pick up girls who were walking down the street, waving them over and inviting them to go for a ride. Heather said she wouldn't get into his Creepmobile if you gave her a thousand bucks.

But the thing was, it didn't feel that creepy to Jimmy. He liked Eddie, and he liked cruising around in the dark with the windows down, listening to Bad Company and Uriah Heep and Deep Purple. He liked the Vega too, and the way he felt when he was inside of it, a guest of honor in the passenger seat. He was always high in there, and that was part of it, that lighter-than-air sensation, like he was floating above the everyday world, where his body weighed a ton and he could barely lift his feet off the ground.

There was something else too, something he had a hard time admitting even to himself—the sense he sometimes had that his mother had arranged it all, that she was the one who'd sent Eddie to rescue him on the night of the wake, to spare him the misery of the funeral home, and give him a place he could go to take a break from the sadness. Sometimes he thought he could sense her presence inside Eddie's car in a way that he no longer could at home, and certainly not at the cemetery, staring down at the rectangle of dirt that was supposedly her resting place.

It was confusing, though, because his mother wouldn't have approved of Eddie if she'd been alive. She would've hated his fast car and his stringy hair, and she would've grounded Jimmy for the rest of his life if she'd found out that he was smoking pot with a high school kid and staying out way past his curfew. But that was the thing—she was dead and the rules were different now, and maybe Eddie and the Vega were the best she could do.

- 4 -

Eddie had a questionable grip on reality. Jimmy understood that pretty quickly. He kept a bottle of gigantic, foul-smelling multivitamins in the glove compartment—he got them mail order from a bodybuilding catalog—and swallowed them dry at random intervals, sometimes several in the course of a single night. He said they turned your piss neon green, but that was how you knew they were working.

I don't really need to eat food, he said. *If I had to, I could just survive on these vitamins.*

I don't think that's true, Jimmy told him.

Eddie looked offended.

What are you, a scientist?

No, are you?

Not really, Eddie admitted. *I guess we'll just have to see which one of us dies first. Loser pays the winner a hundred bucks.*

All right, Jimmy said. *It's a deal.*

They shook hands on it.

You'll be sorry you didn't take your vitamins, Eddie told him.

Another night, they got caught in a thunderstorm so violent that Eddie had to pull over on Marigold Avenue and turn off the engine. The rain was hammering on the roof of the car, and the world turned bright as day with every lightning flash. Eddie popped a vitamin and asked Jimmy if he knew a girl named Cheryl.

Which one? I know like six girls named Cheryl.

The Cheryl I'm talking about is a fox, Eddie said. *But she only has one arm.*

Oh, Jimmy said. *Then no. I don't know any Cheryls with one arm.*

More like one and a half, Eddie said. *The left one just kinda stops at the elbow. Doesn't look that bad. I guess she was born that way.*

Does she live in town?

There was an explosion of light and a thunder crack so loud that it made both of them flinch. After it passed, Eddie removed a joint from his shirt pocket and lit it up, taking a long, slow hit to calm his nerves.

That's what I'm trying to figure out, he said, passing the joint to Jimmy. *I'm driving around one night, and I spot this pretty girl with one arm walking down Chestnut all by herself, so I pull over and ask if she wants to go for a ride, and she's like, sure, and she got in the car and we got stoned and then we parked by the lake and started making out a little. I was feeling her up, and then out of nowhere she reached into my pants and gave me a fucking hand job.*

Really? Jimmy paused for a toke. The rain was softer now, and he lowered his voice after he blew out the smoke. *You just met this girl and she did that?*

Swear to God, Eddie said. *I didn't even mind about the other arm, you know, the half one. She just kinda rested it on my shoulder. I'm telling you, Jimmy. This girl looked like an angel.*

He started the car, and the wipers jumped into frantic motion, slapping across the windshield at full speed. The world looked fresh and clean when he turned them off, the way it always does after a summer storm.

Do you know her last name? Jimmy asked.

Eddie shook his head and put the car into first.

She didn't tell me. I dropped her off and I was like, Hey, Cheryl, could I have your phone number? And she was like, I can't give you my phone number, but you don't need it. I walk around here all the time. Just keep your eye out and you'll find me. Eddie puffed up his cheeks and let them collapse. *That was like three months ago, but I haven't seen her again, and I've been asking around, and nobody's ever heard of a beautiful girl named Cheryl with one arm.*

Maybe you dreamed it, Jimmy told him.

I don't think so, Eddie said, releasing the clutch and pulling away from the curb. *If it was a dream, I think she would've had both arms.*

- 5 -

Eddie went through a lot of pot, all of which he bought at McDonald's. He sent Jimmy in there one night to cop a dime bag, just to show him how easy it was. Jimmy resisted at first, but Eddie guilted him into it.

I'm paying for all of it, he said, *and you're smoking half, so maybe you should start pulling your weight.*

Jimmy reached into his pocket and took out a wad of crumpled bills, a five and three ones.

Here, he said. *I can give you some more tomorrow.*

Keep your money, Eddie told him. *Just go in there and do like I told you. You'll be in and out in two minutes.*

I'm too stoned, Jimmy said. *I'll get paranoid.*

I'm just as stoned as you are, Eddie reminded him. *And don't worry. Leonard's expecting you.*

Leonard was the dealer. Eddie knew him from Auto Shop at the county voc-tech, which he'd attended for a year before transferring to Creamwood High.

How will I know which one is Leonard?

Eddie made a face, like Jimmy was wasting his time.

He'll be the one with the name tag that says Leonard *on it. If there's any doubt, just pick the guy you wouldn't want to get into a fight with.*

It turned out not to be a problem, because there was only one cashier on duty when Jimmy stepped inside, and he didn't look like someone you'd want to get into a fight with. He was also surprisingly handsome, in a square-jawed, tough-guy kind of way.

Jimmy hung back near the doorway, trying his best to look calm and casual. It was nine thirty, just a half hour before closing time, but it was still pretty busy in there, several tables occupied in the dining area, and two customers ahead of him in line. It was bright too, everything bathed in a cheerful fluorescent glow. A bad feeling came over him while he waited, and a very faint voice—the voice of the sensible and responsible person he used to be—spoke up inside of him, telling him that this was a really risky thing to be doing, and that he should just turn around and get the hell out of there. It was good advice, and he might've followed it too, except that the customer in front of him had just finished his transaction, and now it was Jimmy's turn to approach the counter.

Welcome to McDonald's, Leonard said in a bored voice. The brown-and-white uniform looked ridiculous on him, like a Halloween costume. The shirt was way too small for his muscle-bound torso, and the paper hat floated precariously on his puffy hair. *How may I help you?*

Uh . . . Jimmy began, and then he froze. A blond woman in black pants and a white shirt—she must have been the manager—was standing by the apple pie warmer, and he didn't like the way she was looking at him, almost like she knew what he was up to.

How . . . may . . . I . . . help . . . you? Leonard's voice was louder than before, like he thought Jimmy might be hard of hearing.

Just . . . some large fries. If that's okay.

You got it, chief.

Leonard swaggered over to the french fry station and shook some fries into a box with that weird shovel thing they used. By the time he returned to the register, the manager had disappeared into the back. It was now or never.

One more thing, Jimmy added in a shaky voice. *My friend Eddie wants some extra ketchup.*

How much? Leonard said. *One packet or two?*

Jimmy felt a flutter of panic inside his rib cage. He reminded himself to be cool.

I don't know, he said. *The usual, I guess.*

Leonard nodded, like that was fine with him. He reached down and slipped something into the bag, and then he passed the bag across the counter. Jimmy handed him a five and a twenty, Leonard made change for the five, and that was that—it was just as simple as Eddie had told him—except that Jimmy turned around and bumped right into Mr. Kazmierski and his very pregnant wife.

- 6 -

It was always awkward, meeting a teacher outside of school—the stiff chitchat and the fake friendliness, the relief on both sides when it was over—but this was the worst-case scenario.

Well, well, Kaz said with a wry grin. *Fancy meeting you in this fine establishment. Did you get the filet mignon?*

Jimmy forced out a weak chuckle. Kaz was wearing plaid Bermuda shorts and a pistachio-green golf shirt; Jimmy was startled by the carpet of thick black hair on his arms and legs.

Just some french fries, he said, lifting up his bag as proof, and then immediately regretting it.

Kaz nodded his approval.

Best fries in the world. Right, honey?

Mrs. Kazmierski smiled sadly and caressed her gigantic belly. Her shirt was shiny purple with a big white bow at the neck.

I really shouldn't be here, she said. *But this baby loves french fries and vanilla milk shakes.*

Welcome to McDonald's, Leonard called out, an edge of impatience in his voice. *How may I help you?*

Mrs. Kazmierski made a goofy face, like a schoolgirl in trouble with the principal, and headed for the counter. Kaz hung back, studying Jimmy with a sympathetic expression.

How you doing, son?

Pretty good, Jimmy said. He couldn't stop staring at the hair on Kaz's arms, which was almost as dark and thick as the fur on a Labrador retriever, and threatened to engulf his wristwatch. *I'm working at Summer Rec. Helping out with the little kids.*

That's good. Good to keep busy.

I'm just a volunteer, Jimmy explained. His voice sounded peculiar in his own ears, almost robotic. *They gave me a yellow shirt but they don't pay me or anything. It's okay, though. It's pretty cool, you know . . .*

Kaz gave him a funny look. He leaned in a little closer, like a doctor examining a rash.

Are you okay? Your eyes look a little bloodshot.

I'm fine, Jimmy said. *Just hay fever.*

Before Kaz could say anything else, his wife turned and asked him for his wallet. He sighed and reached into his back pocket.

Nice to see you, Jimmy said. He threw a quick wave over his shoulder and darted for the exit. *Have a good summer!*

He wanted to run when he got outside—his heart was jackhammering inside his chest—but he forced himself to walk across the parking lot. He got into the Vega and threw the bag into Eddie's lap.

Thanks a lot, he said. *I almost got busted. My homeroom teacher was in there.*

Oh, noooo! Eddie pretended to cower in fear. *Not your homeroom teacher!*

It's not funny, Jimmy told him, but actually it was, and they spent the rest of the night smoking Leonard's weed and making jokes about a homeroom teacher from hell, an apelike guy with hairy arms who followed you around for the rest of your life, asking why your eyes were so bloodshot, and why your wife wasn't pregnant yet, and why you hadn't died for your country.

THE MYSTIFYING ORACLE

- 1 -

When you're thirteen, you don't know what to think or who to believe. You're just beginning to realize that adults aren't as smart as you thought they were, and a lot of things that had been presented to you as facts your entire life are really just opinions or wishes or half-baked theories, like the idea that dead people go to heaven. The more Jimmy thought about it—the more fervently people insisted that that was where his mother had gone, no question about it—the more skeptical he became. It felt fake—too good to be true—like a story adults had invented to make children feel better and ended up believing themselves. He had his doubts about the Ouija board too, but something about the way Olivia talked about it—like it was a finicky tool that only worked under certain conditions—felt a little more plausible, and made him think it might be worth a try.

The main thing, she explained, was that you couldn't just break it out anytime you felt like it. You needed to do it at night, in a quiet location where no one would bother you. Unfortunately, her own house was out of the question: it wasn't even a house, just a cramped apartment above Poodle Pete's, the dog-grooming shop on Main Street. The place was a mess—she said she'd be embarrassed for Jimmy to even see it—and her mother came and went on an unpredictable schedule, so they couldn't count on any kind of privacy.

And my mother hates the Ouija board, she added. *I have to hide it in a Candy Land box.*

Jimmy said his own house was usually empty at night, but she wasn't comfortable with that option, either. She said she wouldn't be able to relax; she'd just be worried the whole time that his father would come back from the firehouse and find the two of them communing with the spirit world.

He wouldn't like it, she said. *And it'd be even worse if it was your sister.*

No, it wouldn't, Jimmy protested. *Denise is cool. She wouldn't mind.*

If you and I were alone in your house with the lights off? Olivia paused, giving him a moment to visualize the scenario. *I know your sister. She'd think something was going on.*

No way, he said. *She wouldn't think that.*

Olivia gave him a dark look, like he still had a lot to learn.

Trust me, she said. *People think all kinds of crazy things.*

What they needed, she said, was a neutral zone, a hideaway where no one could disturb them because no one would even know they were there.

You know I'm friends with Peg Randowski, right?

Jimmy did know that, because Creamwood was a small town, and because Peg was Janie's sister, though the two of them couldn't have been more different. Where Janie was petite and pretty, Peg was stocky and broad-shouldered, with short hair and a gruff voice that served her well as captain of the girls' field hockey and softball teams.

Olivia wasn't much of an athlete, but she and Peg had gotten close in seventh grade—they were both social misfits and exceptional students—and they'd spent so much time together over the years that Olivia had become an honorary member of the Randowski family. She'd gone on several vacations with them, and had even lived in their house for a few months during the spring of her junior year, when she and her mother weren't getting along. Olivia still had a key to the house, and an open invitation to sleep in the spare room anytime she needed to, even while the Randowskis were out of town for the summer.

It's the perfect place, she said, dangling the key in front of his nose, in case he didn't believe her.

- 2 -

Every teenager in Creamwood knew that the town was full of busybodies and spies, eagle-eyed adults who had nothing better to do than keep track of every pedestrian or car or bicycle that appeared on their street. It was like *1984*, except it wasn't Big Brother who was watching, just some nosy neighbor in an upstairs window who'd probably gone to high school with one of your parents, and would be sure to tell them if they saw you smoking a cigarette or sneaking into the woods or holding hands with a cute girl from Mother Seton. Olivia didn't want the Randowskis to know that she was entertaining visitors while they were away, so she'd instructed Jimmy to wait until night fell and then sneak around to the back patio and enter through the sliding glass doors, which she would leave unlocked.

Don't turn on any lights, she said. *Just come on in.*

It was an unsettling feeling, slipping into Janie's dark house to do something secret and forbidden with Olivia, and he paused for a moment, reminding himself that it wasn't too late to turn around and go home, unwrap a Popsicle, and watch something stupid on TV. But it was just a fleeting thought, because he was here now, and Olivia was waiting, and he didn't want her to think he was a coward.

He was just a little nervous, that was all, because he didn't know her that well and was having some second thoughts about the Ouija board, now that he was on the verge of trying it for the first time. He had no idea how the thing was supposed to work, or what he would say to his mother if it did, except that he loved her and missed her and wished that she wasn't dead, which were things he figured she already knew.

Feeling his way through the darkness, he bumped into a sofa and grunted, more in surprise than pain. The rec room smelled vaguely like Janie—like lemon shampoo and coconut suntan oil—but also a bit musty, like stale flowers and dirty laundry.

The house was a split-level, so he had to climb a short flight of stairs to get to the main living area. There was a welcome glow at the top, the product of two candles burning on the dining room table, one on either side of a Candy Land box. Their flickering light extended into the living room, where Olivia was sitting cross-legged on the couch.

It's me, Jimmy whispered. *I'm here.*

I know, she whispered back. *I can see you.*

He walked past the table and stopped in the archway between the rooms. Olivia patted the cushion beside her.

Come on in, she said. *Don't be a stranger.*

It was a funny thing to say, because she was the one who didn't look like herself. At work she was kind of a slob, messy hair falling into her face, her body lost inside her baggy yellow T-shirt. But here in the candlelight she looked sleek and mature in a long skirt and dark leotard top—it had the planet Saturn silk-screened on the front, its rings frosted with glitter—and her hair pulled back in a tight ponytail.

Jimmy sat down beside her and nodded a silent hello. She took one look at his face and laughed out loud.

Oh my God, she said. *You're scared to death.*

She turned on a lamp, got him a glass of water, and told him that they didn't have to do the Ouija board if he didn't want to. She said she hadn't meant to pressure him, it was just that she'd seen how upset he was, and knew how that felt, losing a parent when you were young, believing that you were permanently separated from someone who loved you. It had been a revelation—such an enormous blessing—the first time she used the board to contact her father.

I can't say for sure if it was really him, she said, *but I think it was, and I felt so much better afterward. I told him about my life and how well I was doing in school, and he said he was proud of me, and I didn't have to worry about him, or about my little brother, because death was a lot more peaceful than people imagined.*

Do you talk to him a lot? Jimmy asked.

No, she said. *Just that once. The board doesn't work when I use it by myself, and it's hard to find someone else to do it with. Peg's too scared, and my other friends act like it's a big joke. That's why I thought that maybe you would be a good person to do it with. But if you're not ready, that's fine. There's no shame in that.*

I'm sorry, Jimmy told her. *I didn't mean to chicken out on you.*

Don't be silly, she said. *It's not a test of your manhood.*

He felt a little more relaxed now that the light was on and he could see her face and they were talking in their regular voices.

You know what? he said. *Maybe you could just show me how it works.*

- 3 -

The board itself was pretty simple—the letters of the alphabet were arrayed in two curving rows, along with the numerals from one to ten (ten was represented by zero), and the words *YES*, *NO*, and *GOOD BYE*.

OUIJA, it read at the top. *THE MYSTIFYING ORACLE.*

Jimmy was more interested in the other piece, the sliding pointer that supposedly moved across the board of its own free will, spelling out messages from the Great Beyond. It was hard plastic, a little smaller than his hand, shaped somewhere between a teardrop and a heart. Olivia rested her fingertips on one side and Jimmy placed his on the other. Their hands were almost touching.

Now what? he asked.

Olivia glanced up from the board. She had taken her granny glasses off, and she looked younger without them, closer to Jimmy's age. Her face was densely freckled, like a sky full of stars.

Now we concentrate, she said. *Think about your mother.*

Jimmy tried to focus, but his eyes kept straying up from the board, drifting past Olivia to a framed photo on the wall behind her, a picture of Janie in her Pop Warner cheerleading outfit. She'd just gotten tossed into the air, and it looked like she was floating crookedly in space, her mouth wide open, her limbs splayed like a starfish.

What's the matter? Olivia asked.

That picture, he said, pointing at the wall. *It's just kinda distracting.*

Olivia turned around and made an exasperated sound.

Jesus, Jimmy.

She got up from her chair, lifted the frame off its hook, and set the photo face down on the table.

There, she said. *Is that better?*

- 4 -

Jimmy had gone on a couple of trout fishing trips with the Celluccis, and the Ouija board reminded him of that, the strange mixture of boredom and suspense, the way you wavered between vague excitement—a sense that something interesting might be about to happen—and the dull certainty that you were wasting your time, your baited hook drifting limply in the current.

It was uncomfortable too, having to sit still and keep his hands in that awkward claw-fingered position. He was about to call a time-out when the pointer jerked suddenly toward the bottom of the board and then scooted back to its original position.

Was that you? he whispered.

Olivia made a shushing sound and swiveled her head toward the living room.

Spirit, she said, her voice sounding deeper and more commanding than usual. *Are you here with us?*

The pointer zigzagged into the upper left quadrant of the board and landed on *YES.* Jimmy hadn't been guiding it, and it didn't seem like Olivia was, either.

Who are you? she asked.

The pointer didn't move, but it felt restless and alive beneath the pads of Jimmy's fingers, humming with energy.

Spirit, Olivia said, *could you please tell us your name?*

After a brief hesitation, the pointer swung in a graceful arc, circling past *NO* and drifting backwards through the number line, all the way to the beginning of the alphabet. It stopped on *B*, the letter Jimmy had been hoping for.

His mother's name was Betty. He could feel her presence in the surrounding air, something warm and familiar, he was almost sure of it.

Mom, he said in a shaky voice. *Is that you?*

The pointer moved again, but this time just a little, stopping briefly at *O* before returning to *B*. Jimmy was confused and disappointed.

Bob? he whispered.

Spirit, Olivia said. *Is your name Bob?*

YES.

She shot a questioning glance at Jimmy, in case he knew a dead person named Bob. Jimmy shrugged and shook his head.

Okay, Bob, Olivia said. *Can I call you Bob? Is that okay?*

U . . . N . . . C . . .

Uncle? she guessed. *Uncle Bob?*

YES.

You're not my uncle, though.

NO.

Uncle Bob, I'm here with my friend, Jimmy. Are you his uncle or great-uncle, or . . .

NO.

Okay, Olivia said. *Then can you please tell us who you are and why you're here?*

There was a pause, almost like the spirit was gathering his thoughts, and then the pointer twitched into action.

L . . . O . . . N . . . E . . .

Lonely? Olivia said. *You're feeling lonely?*

YES.

She made a sympathetic sound.

I'm sorry, Uncle Bob. Is there something we can do to help?

NO.

Olivia frowned, like she wasn't sure what to do next. Jimmy pointed at himself and mouthed the words *My mom.* She nodded, grateful for the reminder.

Uncle Bob, she said. *We're trying to reach a spirit named Betty Perrini from Creamwood, New Jersey. Do you know her?*

NO.

Okay, Olivia said. *Could you do us a favor? If you ever run into Betty, could you please tell her that her son Jimmy sends his love?*

Uncle Bob didn't reply. Jimmy stared at the pointer for a long time, but it was lifeless beneath his fingers. Whatever, or whoever, had been there in the room with them, that presence was gone.

- 5 -

They were quiet afterward, frozen in place, their eyes still trained on the board. Olivia was the first to speak.

That was weird, she said. *I have no idea who that was.*

I thought it was my mom. Jimmy's voice quivered a little, but he steadied himself. *Just for a second. Because of the* B.

I'm sorry. She reached across the table and put her hand on top of his. *Maybe next time.*

It's okay, Jimmy said. He was relieved to have it over and done with. *At least we tried.*

Olivia got up and turned the light on.

We didn't just try, she said. *We actually made contact. A lot of the time nothing happens at all, or the messages you get are complete gibberish. We're a good team, you and me.*

She put the Ouija board and the pointer into the Candy Land box, and hung Janie's picture back on the wall. It was off-kilter at first, but she straightened it out and then pondered it for a few seconds.

I really don't know what you see in her, she said. *I mean, she's cute and everything, but she's such a little airhead.*

Jimmy gave a half-hearted shrug, because Janie was the furthest thing from his mind. He was still a little freaked out by the Ouija board, the way a ghost named Uncle Bob had just popped up out of nowhere and started talking to them.

Do you think they're all lonely? he asked. *The spirits?*

Olivia thought it over, and then shook her head.

No, she said. *Probably not all of them.*

- 6 -

Olivia had decided to crash at the Randowskis' that night, because she enjoyed waking up in a quiet house, and preferred to stay out of her mother's way on the weekends.

She can get a little nasty when she's hung over. Olivia laughed unhappily. She'd put her glasses back on and let her hair out of the ponytail, so she looked a little more like herself. *I wonder who she's gonna yell at after I leave for college. She'll have to get a dog or something.*

She told Jimmy it was okay to leave through the front door, because it was after eleven, and she figured all the neighborhood snoops had gone to bed by then. He followed her down the hall, into a cramped alcove full of shoes and jackets, and waited while she undid the dead bolt. She was frowning when she turned around, like there was something on her mind.

I was just wondering, she said. *Was Janie your first girlfriend?*

Jimmy was annoyed by the question. It was weird enough just being in Janie's house, having to smell her in the air and look at her picture on the wall.

She wasn't really my girlfriend, he said.

Did you kiss her?

Jimmy was surprised by the question.

Just once. He could feel his face getting warm. *After a dance. It wasn't that big a deal.*

It's okay, she said. *It's nothing to be embarrassed about. Nobody knows what they're doing the first few times. I mean, you can't just stick your tongue down a girl's throat.*

I didn't do that, Jimmy said, but then he started to worry. *Did Janie say I did?*

Olivia didn't answer. She leaned down and brought her face even with his.

Why don't you show me how you did it, she said. *Maybe I can give you some pointers.*

He thought she was kidding, so he wasn't ready when she kissed him. His lips were closed and his body was rigid. She pulled away and made a face, like he wasn't being very cooperative.

Come on, she said. *You can do better than that.*

They tried again, and it was a definite improvement. Her tongue was small and pointy, and darted around in surprising ways.

Not bad, she told him. *But you can't just leave your arms hanging down like that. That's not doing anyone any good.*

He placed one hand on her lower back, and the other just above her hip, almost like they were standing on a dance floor, waiting for the music to begin.

Okay, she said. *That's a little better.*

The third kiss lasted a lot longer than the others had. She traced a finger down the middle of his chest and moved her tongue in a swirly motion that he did his best to imitate.

Good, she whispered. She sounded a little breathless. *Now suck on my neck.*

He did what she said, and she must have liked it, because she lifted his hand off her hip and placed it on her breast—he could feel the gritty rings of Saturn under his palm, and the nub of her nipple beneath the fabric—and she let him touch her like that for a little while before she pulled away.

Okay, wow. She stood up to her full height, taking a moment to straighten her eyeglasses and tug the wrinkles out of her shirt. Her face was pink and blotchy, and her eyes were shining. *I think you better go.*

- 7 -

Jimmy walked home in a daze. The night was quiet except for the crickets and the air conditioners and the rubbery slap of his sneakers on the sidewalk.

Have a nice weekend, Olivia had whispered as she hugged him goodbye. *I'll see you on Monday.*

He didn't want to think about Monday, at least not yet. It had been awkward enough, seeing Janie in school on the Monday after the dance, but at least she was his own age and height, and it wasn't completely ridiculous to imagine that they might be a couple. Olivia was six inches taller and two years older than he was, and at the end of the summer she'd be heading off to Drew University on a full scholarship, while Jimmy would be trying to memorize the combination to his new locker at Creamwood High. The idea of the two of them together was too absurd to even think about, or at least he knew it would feel that way at Rec on Monday morning, with all those other people around.

Right now it was still Friday night, and he wanted to keep his mind on that, the way her breathing had changed when he kissed her neck, the shocking softness of her breast, and the flustered blush on her face when they'd separated, because even if the whole thing had started out as a lesson—or even a joke—that wasn't how it had ended. He made up his mind to call her the moment he got home—he knew the Randowskis' phone number by heart—and tell her . . . *something*. Maybe that he already missed her. Or maybe just how happy he was, and then she would say, *Why are you so happy?* and he would say, *You know why*, and they would take it from there.

His body was humming the whole way back to Morgan Street, and he kept reciting Janie's phone number in his head, because that was the number he was going to dial as soon as he got inside his house, and he was halfway across the lawn before he even noticed the stranger sitting at the bottom of his front stoop.

Oh God, Jimmy blurted, partly because he was caught off guard, but mostly because the stranger was Black. Without thinking, he raised his hands, as if the man were holding a gun. *You're not supposed to be here.*

Take it easy now, the stranger said, keeping his voice low and calm. There was a gym bag resting between his feet. *It's cool.*

The guy seemed nice enough, and Jimmy felt like a fool with his hands in the air, so he lowered them to his sides.

Can I help you? he asked.

I hope so, the stranger said. He sounded a little worried. *I'm looking for a lady named Nilda. I thought she stayed here.*

Oh. Jimmy released the breath he'd been holding and pointed at Wayne's house. *Nilda's right next door. Three twenty-three. This is three twenty-one.*

The stranger stood up and grabbed his gym bag. He was a skinny young guy with a medium-sized Afro, dressed in bell bottoms and a tight-fitting shirt.

Didn't mean to startle you, little man. He gave Jimmy a friendly nod and headed off in the direction of Wayne and Nilda's. *You have a good night now.*

You too, Jimmy said, and he climbed the front steps and went into his empty house. He thought again about calling Olivia, but it was almost midnight, and he was suddenly very tired, and just wanted to go straight to bed.

The Ouija board must have unnerved him more than he realized, because he stayed awake for quite a while, and for some reason he kept thinking about a night in the Lenape Park woods—it was two summers ago, right after his mother's first operation—when he held on to a lit cherry bomb for a half second too long, and it almost exploded in his hand.

I've reached the age where I sometimes think about my own obituary—how I'll be remembered, or if I'll be remembered at all, beyond the small circle of my family and friends.

"Jay Perry," the headline might say, if it's a slow news day, and I'm lucky enough to claim some space on the bottom third of an inside page in the *Times*. *"Author and Creator of Heartwarming Series for Young Viewers."*

That's the best I can hope for, and it bothers me to imagine it, because I never set out to make a TV show for kids. For most of my career, I was a writer of literary fiction—a serious novelist, or so I liked to tell myself—trying to eke out a living while keeping faith with my artistic ideals.

I did have a few modest successes. My debut coming-of-age novel, *Orphan Song*, was published when I was thirty-seven, after a decade of rejection. It tells the story of thirteen-year-old Ricky Farrentino, a working-class kid from New Jersey whose parents die in a car accident in chapter one. An only child, Ricky gets adopted by his Uncle Jonathan, a closeted jazz pianist who lives in a run-down one-bedroom apartment in Greenwich Village. They're wary of each other at first, but a bond slowly develops between them as Jonathan introduces Ricky to the music he loves, and begins to open up about his sexuality, which he's had to keep hidden from his homophobic Italian American family for his entire life. The novel takes place during the early years of the AIDS epidemic, a dark cloud hovering over the action, threatening Jonathan's life and Ricky's hard-won sense of security and belonging.

Orphan Song's been out of print for a long time, but for what it's worth, the *Washington Post* called it "a bildungsroman of great sensitivity and compassion, and an eloquent plea for tolerance," and *Newsday* said I was "a writer to watch." A studio optioned the book and scripts were written (not by me), but the material was "tricky"—not a lot of gay characters on the screen in those days—and the movie never got made. It was okay, though; we used the option money for a down payment on our first house, and Molly fully supported my decision to quit my job as a prep school English teacher and try to make a go of it as a full-time writer.

I followed *Orphan Song* with a collection of short fiction—*Misty's Mom and Other Tales from Suburbia*—that I still consider my best work. I'm especially proud of the title story, which is narrated by a guy named Ted, a thirtysomething dad dying of boredom at a birthday party for kindergartners. While a sweaty middle-aged clown named Mr. Boogers entertains the kids, Ted strikes up a conversation with a vivacious woman he's never seen before, who introduces herself only as "Misty's mom." They bond over the misery of yet another wasted Saturday, and eventually sneak upstairs to make out in the birthday girl's bedroom while Mr. Boogers leads the kids in a sing-along.

Their sexual chemistry is immediate and explosive, but they don't get very far. There's some kind of emergency downstairs, people yelling at one another to call 911. Misty's mom rushes off in alarm, and Ted follows a moment later. It's pandemonium in the living room, kids wailing and adults looking shocked, and Mr. Boogers motionless on the floor, receiving futile CPR from a firefighter dad until the ambulance arrives and takes his body away.

Ted loses track of Misty's mom in the chaos, and can't stop thinking about her in the days that follow. He asks around at the school playground, but none of the other parents have any idea who he's talking about. At the supermarket one evening, he runs into Marcia, the host of the party, and repeats his inquiry. Marcia stares at him in bewilderment. She says that a little girl named Misty used to live in her house, but that she'd moved to North Carolina eight years ago. Marcia and her husband had bought the house from Misty's dad.

"But Misty's mom was at your party," Ted says. "I had a nice conversation with her."

"What are you talking about?" Marcia says. "Misty's mom is dead. She was sleepwalking one night and fell down the stairs. That was why they moved. They couldn't stand being in the house after that."

The story ends with Ted at the cemetery. He's standing beneath an umbrella on a cold rainy day, staring at a headstone that reads *Linda T. Giroux, Loving Wife of Henry, Devoted Mother of Misty Lee, Taken Too Soon.* He says a prayer for Misty's mom, places a bouquet of flowers on the grass, and starts walking back to his car. On the way, he spots another mourner, a woman in full clown regalia—fright wig and red nose and gigantic shoes—standing by a freshly dug grave. Ted heads over to join her, sheltering her with his umbrella while she weeps for Mr. Boogers.

I used to tell people that I had two different writing careers, one for love and one for money, but I don't believe that anymore. The truth is, it's all been one thing, just a bunch of variations on the only themes that have ever mattered to me.

Ghosts and Orphans.

Orphans and Ghosts.

The ways we're abandoned and never left alone.

SALTWATER SKY

- 1 -

It must have been Denise who invited Father Paul for a cookout in the backyard, because it wasn't Jimmy, and Jimmy was pretty sure it wasn't his dad, though it was also possible that Father Paul had invited himself. Priests could do that back then, even the younger ones.

So how are the Perrinis? he asked, after he'd thanked the Lord for these, Thy gifts. He was wearing the clerical version of street clothes, black pants and a black short-sleeved shirt with the white collar. *I haven't seen some of you in a while.*

Jimmy and his father traded uncomfortable glances. They'd been regular churchgoers before his mother had gotten sick—his mother had made sure of it—but their attendance had become sporadic in the past year, and neither one of them had set foot in Our Lady since the funeral. Denise was the only one who'd been making an effort on Sunday mornings, faithfully attending the ten thirty folk mass. It was Father Paul's baby; he chose all the songs and sometimes even strummed them on his twelve-string acoustic, though Denise said he wasn't nearly as good as Joey O'Connor, the regular guitarist, who was locally famous for singing in a David Bowie cover band with a red-and-blue lightning bolt painted across his face.

All the Perrinis said they were doing okay. Denise talked about her babysitting job, Jimmy described his duties as a junior counselor at Rec, and their father said he was busting his hump fabricating ductwork for the new A&P they were building on the site of the old furnace factory.

Big job, he said. *Tons of overtime. I'm beat on the weekends. And then I got the fire department on top of that.*

What about vacation? Father Paul asked. *Are you gonna get a break? Maybe head down the shore?*

The question caught all three of them by surprise. The truth was, they hadn't discussed any kind of summer getaway; it had never even occurred to them. Vacation was Jimmy's mother's job—deciding where to go and what to do for fun and how they'd be able to afford it. Her preference had always been for short trips to sites of historical interest—Sturbridge Village, Colonial Williamsburg, the whaling ships at Mystic Seaport—but she liked amusement parks too, and had promised more than once that they would all go to the new Disney World in Florida when she was feeling a little better. Now that she was gone, it was hard for Jimmy to imagine the three of them ever loading up the station wagon and heading off on a trip to anywhere, ever again, which was exactly how it turned out.

Maybe not this year, Jimmy's father said. *You know, out of respect for Betty.*

Father Paul nodded, but he looked a little skeptical, like he wasn't sure how avoiding the beach was a sign of respect for the dead.

What about you, Father? Denise asked. *Do priests ever go on vacation?*

Jimmy thought that was an interesting question, and one he never would've dared to ask, because he'd somehow gotten the impression that you weren't allowed to ask priests about their private lives.

I'm not sure I'd call it a vacation. Father Paul picked up his burger with both hands. *I'm going on a retreat at the end of the month. There's a monastery up in Maine, right on the coast. Beautiful place. Nothing like the Jersey Shore. The beach is just a big rock pile.*

Denise nodded like a bobblehead doll, her eyes wide with fascination. She had a talent for looking interested.

What's that like, Father? What do you do on a retreat?

Father Paul held up one finger while he finished chewing.

You pray a lot, he said. *And you reflect on your relationship with God. This is a very good hamburger, by the way.*

Are you allowed to talk? Denise asked.

In moderation. Father Paul ate a forkful of potato salad and politely shielded his mouth while he spoke. *And only when you have something essential to communicate. It's about removing the distractions, and trying to hear the Lord's voice in the silence.*

No offense, Jimmy's father said, *but that doesn't sound like much of a vacation.*

None taken, Father Paul assured him. *It's not everyone's cup of tea. For what it's worth, though, I do try to swim in the ocean whenever I can find the time. The water's freezing up there, but it's really invigorating. And I know it might sound a little mystical, but I'm always very conscious of God's presence when I'm near the ocean. It's been that way ever since I was a kid down in Wildwood.*

That's a nice beach, Jimmy's father said.

Father Paul's face grew wistful, like he was watching a movie in his head.

My grandparents had a shack down there, he said. *We went every August. My dad used to get up at the break of dawn and take a long swim in the ocean. When I was nine or ten, I started going with him. That was heaven for me, just the two of us out in the water.*

Denise was nodding and smiling, but Jimmy's dad looked upset, like Father Paul's story had hurt his feelings. He turned to Jimmy with a wounded expression.

You love the beach, he said in a soft voice. *Always did, ever since you were little.*

It's fun, Jimmy agreed, though in truth he could take it or leave it. It was always an ordeal to get down the shore, fighting weekend traffic in a hot car, looking for a place to park that wasn't too far from the beach. He always came home cranky and stinking of Coppertone, with water in his ears and sand in his crotch. It was different for people like Janie, who had summer houses and didn't have to drive all the way back to Creamwood at the end of the day.

We'll get back down there, his father said. *I promise.*

It's okay, Jimmy told him. *There's no rush.*

No. It's not okay. Jimmy's dad made a frustrated sound, and turned to Father Paul. *I'm just working too much. It's hard to pass up the overtime.*

Of course, Father Paul said. *You have to support your family. But maybe you could—*

He stopped there, because that was when Wayne and Nilda came out of their back door and wandered over to the chain-link fence to say hello.

Hey there. Wayne stopped and sniffed the air, hamming it up a bit. *Something smells good.*

Jimmy's dad seemed relieved by the interruption.

Just a little cookout, he said. *We can throw a few more burgers on the grill if you want to join us.*

That's kind of you, Wayne said. *But we're all set.*

While he was saying this, the back door popped open, and the Black guy who had surprised Jimmy on Friday night came down the stairs and headed over to the fence. Nilda cleared her throat and nodded at the new arrival.

Hey, everybody, she said. *I want you to meet my cousin Hector.*

Hector raised his hand in a shy gesture of greeting. In the waning daylight, Jimmy could see that he was only a year or two older than Denise, and that he looked a lot like Nilda, though his skin was darker than hers.

Hector, Nilda continued, *that's Uncle Frank and Denise and Jimmy, and um . . .*

Father Dannehy, said Father Paul.

Nice to meet you, Hector said, and then he gave Jimmy a special nod and finger point. *Good to see you, little man.*

Normally Jimmy would have bristled at the nickname, but Hector said it in such a good-humored way that it didn't seem like a put-down.

You too, Jimmy said, and he could feel everyone puzzling over this exchange, wondering how it was that he and Hector were already acquainted.

Hector's gonna be staying with us for a little while, Wayne said. *Just wanted to give you a heads-up.*

Whoa, Jimmy's father said, and Jimmy could hear the surprise and displeasure in his voice. *For how long?*

Hard to say. Wayne put one arm around Nilda's shoulders and the other around Hector's. *We're gonna play it by ear.*

No one had a camera that evening, but Jimmy remembered it like a faded snapshot, the three of them standing by the fence, looking impossibly young and beautiful: Wayne in the middle, with his Jesus hair and beard; Hector on the right, with his puffy Afro and clingy shirt; and Nilda on the left, with her wild ringlets and a worried smile, as if she could sense some ominous vibrations in the air, but wasn't sure where they were coming from.

- 2 -

The three of them headed down the driveway, got into the Beetle, and drove away. Everyone was silent around the picnic table for a few seconds, each of them waiting for somebody else to say something. It was Jimmy's father who finally broke the ice.

Jesus Christ, he said, and Jimmy could hear how shaken he was. *That's her cousin?*

It's not that big a thing, Denise told him. *He's just visiting.*

Yeah, right, Jimmy's father said. *Tell that to the neighbors.*

They were quiet again. No one seemed to know if they should keep talking about Hector, return to the conversation they were having before, or move on to a new topic. Father Paul rapped the table softly with his knuckle.

You know what? he said. *I can take Jimmy to the beach.*

What? Jimmy's dad looked startled, and then he shook his head. *No, no, Father. That's not your job.*

It's not a job, Father Paul told him. *It would be my pleasure. I know you've got a lot to deal with right now, and I'm happy to pick up some slack.*

He sounded sincere, and Jimmy's father gave a shrug of surrender.

That's very kind of you, he said, and then he turned to Jimmy. *Whaddaya think?*

If Jimmy had been alone with his dad, he would have said that he wasn't crazy about the idea. He didn't dislike Father Paul, but he couldn't imagine sitting in a car with him for two hours, talking about monks and retreats and why God didn't want us to touch ourselves, or hanging out with him on the beach, the two of them side by side on a blanket. But there was no way to say that out loud, not when Father Paul was right across the table.

Uh . . . when would this be? he asked.

Saturday, said Father Paul. *I have to work on Sunday.*

Jimmy's father and Denise thought that was pretty funny.

Sure, Jimmy said, without a lot of enthusiasm. *I guess that would be okay.*

Excellent. Father Paul gave him a subtle nod, like they were pals now. *I'll see you bright and early.*

- 3 -

Father Paul pulled up in front of Jimmy's house at seven o'clock sharp on Saturday morning in a beige Lincoln Continental with a black vinyl roof. The seats were real leather and there was an impressive amount of legroom up front, way more than Jimmy needed.

Morning, said Father Paul. *Looks like we picked ourselves a beautiful day.*

He was wearing flip-flops and navy blue shorts and a gray sweatshirt with *Fordham* written across the front. Jimmy had never seen him out of uniform and was surprised by how normal he looked.

I'm off duty, he said. *I can wear whatever I want.*

Jimmy didn't say so, but he was deeply relieved. He'd been dreading the prospect of walking onto the beach alongside a priest dressed in black, as if he were some kind of pathetic orphan or charity case.

Did you eat some breakfast? Father Paul asked as they pulled away.

Just a bowl of Cap'n Crunch, Jimmy said.

Huh. Father Paul made a face, like he was sorry to hear it. *I'm more of a Count Chocula guy myself.*

Father Paul wasn't a daredevil behind the wheel, but he wasn't timid, either. The real weekend traffic hadn't started up yet, so there was still some room to maneuver on the Parkway. When he needed to, he was happy to punch the gas and swing into the left lane, blowing past the slowpokes in the middle.

Your car's got some pickup, Jimmy said.

It sure does. But it's not my car. It's the monsignor's. He lets me borrow it sometimes.

Jimmy was surprised to hear it. Monsignor Blevins didn't seem like the kind of guy who'd let you drive his fancy car to the beach.

That's nice of him.

It's very generous, Father Paul agreed, but then he frowned, like something wasn't quite right. *The monsignor only drives brand-new Lincolns. He does a trade-in every year. It's a gift from his family, but . . . I don't know, Jimmy. How do you square a car like this with a vow of poverty?*

Jimmy didn't have an opinion on that, so he just shrugged and started messing around with the power window, which was still a novelty to him at the time.

Is it too hot? Father Paul asked. *We can put on the AC if you want.*

No, it's fine. Jimmy closed the window and turned back to face the road. *It's just, my hair was blowing in my eyes.*

Father Paul nodded and patted his bald spot.

Not a big problem for me, he said.

- 4 -

It wasn't even nine o'clock when they got to the beach, and there were only a handful of people camped out on the vast stretch of sand between the boardwalk and the ocean. The lifeguard chairs were deserted, and the rides on Casino Pier—the Jet Star and the Zipper and the Scrambler and the Ferris wheel and all the rest—were completely still, like a life-sized postcard. In a few hours, Seaside would be wall-to-wall bodies and Frisbees and blaring radios, but right then it was just foaming whitecaps and shrieking gulls, light-blue sky and glittering dark-blue water. Jimmy felt like he'd never seen the ocean before, not like this, and had never really understood how relentless it was, the way the waves kept crashing into the shore, one after the other after the other, and would never stop until the world came to an end.

Father Paul didn't mess around. He took a moment to spread out their blanket, anchoring the corners with his flip-flops and Jimmy's sneakers, and then he got undressed—he was wearing a bathing suit under his shorts—and ran straight into the surf, diving headfirst into a breaking wave. Jimmy took a more gradual approach, hugging himself and whimpering as he waded into the chilly water.

Usually he just bobbed around in the ocean, riding the swells and ducking beneath the breakers, but Father Paul showed him how to bodysurf, which was a lot more fun. The waves were ideal that morning—strong, but not too big or unpredictable—and it was easier than he expected. He followed Father Paul's lead, waddling against the tide to get into position, and then turning to face the shore.

Wait, Father Paul would say. *Wait . . . wait . . . now!*

At the signal, they'd fling themselves forward, pushing off with their feet. If they timed it right, their bodies would merge with the wave, and for a few seconds they'd be weightless, arms outstretched, twin supermen hurtling through a saltwater sky, the sea roaring in their ears, until gravity slapped them down and they were themselves again, gliding through the foamy aftermath, laughing as they peeled themselves up from the sandy bottom. Then they'd trudge back out and do it again, over and over, until they were wiped out and needed to go lie down for a while.

They repeated this cycle several times, until there were too many people in the water and it wasn't fun anymore, and then they rinsed off at an outdoor shower, changed into dry clothes, and headed to the boardwalk for lunch. It was weird being there in the daytime—a little sad—without the flashing lights and loud music, nobody shooting BB guns at paper targets or crashing bumper cars. They ate pizza and frozen custard, and then they ducked into a dimly lit arcade, playing game after game of pinball and Skee-Ball, hiding themselves from the midday sun until it was time to go home.

- 5 -

There was an accident on the Parkway, and they got stuck in a huge traffic jam, one of those epic standstills where people get out of their cars and start chatting with strangers right there on the highway, everybody standing on tiptoe and craning their necks, trying to see what the hold-up was. Some young guys broke out a six-pack and offered Father Paul a beer, which he politely declined. A frustrated middle-aged man climbed onto the roof of his car to get a better look, but all he saw were some flashing lights in the far distance. They were stopped for over half an hour, and when they finally got moving again, Jimmy really had to pee.

Father, he said. *If you don't mind stopping at the next rest area . . .*

No problem, said Father Paul. *I was thinking the exact same thing.*

Needing a bathroom when you're stuck in highway traffic is one of those everyday tortures—like stomach cramps or toothaches—that your memory just erases once the crisis is over. All Jimmy could recall was that he and Father Paul were both in bad shape when they finally made it to the rest stop. There was a line for the men's room, of course—it was a summer Saturday—and they had to fidget and grit their teeth until two side-by-side urinals happened to become available at the exact same moment.

It felt like a synchronized dance routine, the two of them stepping forward and unzipping in unison, and heaving dramatic sighs as they let loose. There was a moment of exquisite relief, and then Father Paul nudged Jimmy with his elbow.

Praise Jesus, he whispered, and they both started cracking up, which wasn't great for their aim.

- 6 -

Jimmy forgot about that day for a long time, and didn't think about it again until decades later, when everything started coming out about Catholic priests and the terrible things they'd done to so many kids. It made him wonder about Father Paul, if maybe he'd been one of the bad ones, if his reasons for taking Jimmy down the shore weren't entirely innocent.

All he could say in the end was that Father Paul hadn't done anything wrong, hadn't touched him or said anything creepy or inappropriate. He brought Jimmy home and shook his hand, and said that he hoped to see him in church one of these days. Then he drove off in the monsignor's Continental, leaving Jimmy alone on the sidewalk in front of his house, his mind empty, his body glowing with that peaceful, washed-out feeling you get after a really good day at the beach.

FANTABULOUS NIGHT

- 1 -

It was the annual paradox of summer, the way the days took their sweet time, and the season passed so quickly. The Fourth of July firecrackers had barely gone quiet and suddenly it was August, a fact Jimmy knew all too well, because everyone around him kept mentioning it with a kind of melancholy wonder, like the calendar couldn't possibly be right, like maybe someone had pulled a fast one.

Is it really August?

No fuckin' way it's August already.

Where'd the summer go?

It wasn't just the month that had changed. The weather turned unpleasantly hot and sticky, and people got cranky, and things started going wrong. Just little things, at first, like the morning Jimmy got turned away from Rec's one and only field trip of the summer because he didn't have a permission slip. It wasn't that he forgot, he just didn't think he needed one. It was humiliating, because Doug had to remind him that he wasn't actually a counselor, despite what it said on his shirt.

I'm sorry, he said. *You can't get on the bus without a valid signature from a parent or guardian.*

It's not fair, Jimmy said. *No one told me and my mom's not home.*

He saw the startled look on Doug's face and corrected himself.

I mean, my dad, he said, though he couldn't imagine his father signing a permission slip. That had been another one of his mother's jobs. *He's not home, either.*

Doug gave him a consoling pat on the shoulder.

Just take the day off and enjoy yourself. You're not missing anything, believe me.

Jimmy didn't care about the field trip itself—it was just some kind of ethnic dance festival at the Garden State Arts Center, a full day of people in traditional costumes clomping around to music no one wanted to hear. It was the bus ride he'd been looking forward to, being out on the highway with his friends, singing "A Hundred Bottles of Beer on the Wall," playing the Name Game and Twenty Questions. And he felt even worse when Olivia pulled him aside and told him how disappointed she was, because she'd been hoping they could sit together.

Who am I supposed to talk to? she said.

I don't know, he said. *Heather? You guys are friends, right?*

She made a face, like that was news to her. She'd gotten dressed up for the trip—ballet slippers and a patchwork skirt—and had even tied a knot in the front of her yellow T-shirt, so it fit a lot better than usual.

I wish I could just stay here with you, she told him.

He was surprised to hear it, because she'd been a little cool to him in the two weeks that had passed since their Ouija session. Not unfriendly, exactly, but a little more distant and reserved—no more touching his hand with paintbrushes, or secret glances at the lunch table, and no more invitations to meet up at Janie's house. It had stung for a day or two, but it was also a relief, because their encounter with the spirit world had troubled him more than he wanted to admit, and he had no desire to repeat it.

That would be fun, he said. *But what would we do all day?*

In the parking lot, the kids were all lined up, waiting to board the school bus. Nick and Doug were taking attendance, counting heads and checking names off a list.

I don't know. She gave a cryptic shrug, like she had a few ideas that she wasn't quite ready to share. *I'm sure we'd think of something.*

And then she got on the bus with everyone else and they all drove off without him.

- 2 -

Jimmy had nowhere else to go—it was only ten in the morning—so he got back on his bike and rode home. He ate a big bowl of Cap'n Crunch, and headed upstairs for his second shower of the day. When he was done, he wandered over to his bedroom window, still dripping a little.

It wasn't prime sunbathing time, so he was pleasantly surprised to see that Nilda was out in the yard, until he looked again and realized that it was Hector who was lying on the Budweiser beach towel. He was flat on his back in a pair of plaid swim trunks that were too big for him, a glass of orange juice and a portable radio resting on the grass near his head.

Hector couldn't possibly have seen Jimmy in the window, but he must have sensed that he was being watched. He sat up and looked around, as if maybe someone had just called his name, and he couldn't get comfortable after that. He tried a few different positions, but none of them lasted very long, and then he gathered up his stuff and went inside.

- 3 -

In the afternoon Jimmy biked over to the basketball court behind the junior high school, a popular gathering spot for guys his own age. It was the first time he'd been back since graduation, and the building seemed smaller and less imposing than he remembered, a place meant for kids much younger than himself. He was especially embarrassed by the feel-good mural on the back wall—he'd helped paint it the previous summer—a chain of rainbow-colored paper doll silhouettes, each one with a letter on its chest, spelling out the message *WE LIVE AND LEARN!*

He felt a little nervous climbing off his bike, showing up out of the blue after such a long absence, but he received a warmer welcome than he expected, like his old friends wanted him to know that they'd missed him, and were happy have him back where he belonged. They laughed at his *COUNSELOR* shirt and spent a few minutes teasing him about his Rec job, which, in their telling, required him to spend his days wiping asses and teaching ballet to a bunch of little brats, and then they moved on to more pressing subjects, like how fucking hot it was, and how pathetic it was that Creamwood was the only town in the entire county too cheap to have a public swimming pool, which was where they all would have spent their afternoons if they'd had any kind of choice in the matter, doing backflips and cannonballs off a high dive while pretty girls in bikinis judged them from the sidelines, holding up cardboard signs with numbers on them.

It was just like old times, except that Greg Cellucci was there, and Jimmy wasn't about to pretend that everything was cool between them. They greeted each other with grudging nods, and did their best to avoid unnecessary eye contact, though Jimmy couldn't help noticing how tan Greg was, and how much taller and older he looked, like he'd gone through a growth spurt over the past couple of weeks. He'd had a wispy mustache and some half-assed sideburns the last time Jimmy had seen him, but all that was gone now, which meant that he must have started shaving, and Jimmy couldn't help feeling like he was being left behind, losing a race that he hadn't even signed up for.

That sense of unfairness only intensified when they got out on the basketball court. They played three on three, Shirts vs. Skins, and Jimmy had the unenviable job of guarding Greg. They'd both been starters in junior high, but Greg had always been the better player, and he'd been practicing hard over the summer, upping his game, while Jimmy had been smoking weed with Eddie and losing to six-year-olds at Ping-Pong. He was slow and rusty, and Greg faked him out three times in a row, scoring one easy bucket after another.

He tightened up his defense after that, gluing himself to Greg like a cheap suit, as Coach Hansen used to say, bumping him with his chest and slapping at his hands, and tugging on his shirt to slow him down. Greg called two fouls in a row, and glared at Jimmy in frustration.

Why are you being such a dick? he asked.

There's only one dick here, Jimmy told him, *and I'm pretty sure it's not me.*

Some of the other guys laughed, and Greg got pissed. He tried to drive to the net, but Jimmy stayed with him, forcing him into a bad shot that caromed off the back of the rim. Greg used his height advantage to grab the rebound, swinging his elbow in a wild arc that caught Jimmy square in the mouth and sent him sprawling backwards on his ass.

He sat on the ground for a little while, too stunned to speak. He tasted blood, but his mouth didn't hurt as much as he thought it would, and all of his teeth were still where they were supposed to be. Greg crouched down and tried to assess the damage.

I'm sorry, he said, and it sounded like he meant it. *That was an accident. I swear to God.*

He offered a helping hand, but Jimmy swatted it away and stood up on his own.

I'm fine, he said. *Let's just finish the damn game.*

He played better after that, but his team still lost. When it was over, Greg apologized again, and Jimmy told him to forget about it. Greg hesitated, like there was something else he wanted to say.

What? Jimmy said.

Greg ran his hand through his hair. He looked a little embarrassed.

My mom misses you, he said. *She keeps asking why you never come over anymore.*

Jimmy didn't know what to say to that. Mrs. Cellucci had been really good to him when his mom got sick, inviting him for dinner once or twice a week, and always sending him home with trays of lasagna or baked ziti or homemade cookies for his family. She'd cried really hard at the wake, and then she'd sent two condolence cards to the house, one for his father and Denise, and the other just for Jimmy.

Your mother didn't leave you, she wrote. *She'll always be right there in your heart whenever you need her.*

The card had meant a lot to him—he still had it in his sock drawer—and Jimmy had meant to thank her, but he couldn't imagine calling her on the phone, or even writing a note. He just figured that he'd run into her somewhere, but that hadn't happened, and now it felt like the moment had passed.

Tell her I'm sorry. Jimmy looked at his feet. *It's been a weird summer.*

- 4 -

He iced his mouth when he got home, but it was too late. His top lip was already puffy and tender, pooching out like the overhang of a roof. Eddie noticed it right away when Jimmy got into the Vega that evening. Their nighttime drives had become a ritual, and they'd started going farther afield to keep things interesting—Sandy Hook and Asbury Park, South Mountain Reservation and the Menlo Park Mall, where you could cool off in the air-conditioning and watch the people go by.

Holy shit, he said. *What happened to you?*

Nothing. Just caught an elbow playing hoops.

Who from?

Jimmy shrugged, like it was just a stupid coincidence.

Cellucci.

What? Eddie knew all about Jimmy's rivalry with Greg, and thought Jimmy should've done something about it a long time ago. *I hope you punched his lights out.*

It was an accident. We were both going for the ball.

Yeah, Eddie said. *And I guess it's just an accident when he fucks your girlfriend.*

They're not doing that, Jimmy said. *She wouldn't . . .*

How do you know? Eddie asked. *Were you like, Excuse me, old buddy. I was just wondering if you and sweet little Janie had ever—*

You know what? Jimmy said. *Why don't we change the subject.*

Suit yourself. I'm just trying to help.

Eddie wasn't usually such a jerk, but he'd run out of pot three days ago—apparently the whole tristate area had run out of pot—and it was taking a toll on his nerves. He'd contacted everyone he could think of, but no one had anything to sell, not even a loose joint of shitty Mexican dirtweed. He said he'd spent his whole afternoon combing through the Vega, and had only found two roaches and three or four seeds, which he'd smoked along with some resin he'd scraped out of a pipe, but he couldn't even catch a buzz.

Did you try Leonard? Jimmy asked.

Of course I tried Leonard. I called him first thing this morning. He said he'd have something tonight, so I went to McDonald's but he didn't have shit, because Shirley's kid got sick and she had to take the night off.

Shirley was the manager lady from McDonald's, the one who'd scared Jimmy the first time he bought weed from Leonard, which Eddie thought was hilarious, because it was Shirley's weed that Leonard was selling.

Shirley has a kid? Jimmy asked.

Yeah, like a two-year-old or something.

So . . . she's married?

I doubt it, Eddie said. *I don't think she'd be blowing Leonard every night if she was married.*

Are you serious? Jimmy was having trouble fitting all the pieces together. *She's Leonard's girlfriend? Isn't she like thirty?*

I don't know how old she is, Eddie said. *And she's not his* girlfriend. *They just get high sometimes and mess around.*

Is Leonard the kid's father?

Jesus Christ, you ask a lot of questions.

I'm just curious.

Well, you know what? You can ask her yourself, 'cause we're going over there tonight after Leonard's done with his shift.

- 5 -

Shirley lived in South Drumford, which Jimmy's father always said was *a tough town*, even though it looked exactly like Creamwood. Leonard lived there too, and he didn't have a great opinion of the place.

It's your basic shithole, he told them on the way. *Just a bunch of ________s and Deadheads. I don't know which is worse.*

Jimmy wasn't surprised by the racial slur. It was always floating around in the air of his childhood, like the secondhand smoke and asbestos particles no one worried about, either.

What's wrong with the Dead? Eddie asked. *"Casey Jones" is a cool song.*

That one's okay, Leonard agreed, a little grudgingly. *But don't give me any of that "Uncle John's Band" crap. And don't ask me to paint my face, either. You ever watch those fuckers dance? It's like they never even saw their own hands before.*

That's 'cause they're tripping, Eddie said.

Bullshit. I've taken tons of acid and I never danced like an asshole. Leonard shook his head like he'd just received some sad news.

You know what? I'd rather listen to _______ music than the Grateful Dead. Gimme Sly and the Family Stone any day.

Eddie nodded, happy to find some common ground.

Sly's great. He lowered his voice, and did a pretty good imitation. *It's a family aff-air-hair, it's a family aff-air-hair.*

Leonard turned around and looked at Jimmy, who'd been relegated to the back seat.

What about you, Jack? What kind of music do you like?

Jimmy didn't know Leonard very well—they'd only hung out once before, and only long enough to smoke a joint—so he wasn't sure if *Jack* was a nickname or an honest mistake, and didn't bother to correct it.

Mostly hard rock, he said. *Zeppelin, Sabbath, Aerosmith. Stuff like that. Jethro Tull.*

Leonard had been nodding along with the list, but the final item made him gag in disbelief.

C'mon, he said. *Jethro Tull?*

What? You don't like Tull?

Leonard pretended to think it over.

Tell you what, he said. *I might like him a little better if he took that flute and shoved it up his ass.*

- 6 -

Jimmy wasn't sure how much money a McDonald's manager earned, but he was startled when they pulled to a stop in front of a run-down house with a missing shutter on one of the front windows and grass that badly needed mowing, the kind of place his father would have called an *eyesore*. The neighboring homes were no bigger, but they were neater and better tended, one with a nice-looking birdbath out front, and another with a statue of a lifelike deer that appeared to be grazing on the lawn.

Is this really Shirley's house? he asked.

She just rents it, Leonard told him. *The landlord's an asshole.*

Jimmy was nervous about going inside, but happy to get out of the car. He'd felt queasy and confined in the back seat; the air had seemed weirdly thick back there, almost like a separate atmosphere—*close*, his mother would have called it—and he'd been aware of an unpleasant odor, something sweet and vaguely rancid that might have been emanating from some old fast-food bags on the floor.

You guys keep your mouth shut, Leonard told them as they headed up the front walk. *Let me do the talking.*

Jimmy had assumed they were invited guests, but Leonard had to ring the bell three times, and Shirley didn't look too happy when she finally appeared at the door.

What are you doing here? she asked.

Just came to say hi, Leonard said. *Is it a bad time?*

It's late, Shirley told him, and Jimmy could hear the irritation in her voice. *My kid is sick.*

It's not that late. It's only ten thirty.

I've been up since five in the morning, Leonard. I'm exhausted.

Sorry, he said. *I didn't know. Just roll us a joint and we'll get out of your hair.*

She craned her neck and looked around before she spoke. Her voice was quieter than before, like she was worried about the neighbors.

I don't have anything, Leonard.

What are you talking about? You said it was coming today.

There's some kind of delay. And I really don't want to get into this right now. So why don't you and your friends get back in your car and let me get some sleep. I'll tell you more at work tomorrow.

Sure. It's just . . . Leonard placed his hand on Jimmy's shoulder. *I was telling my buddy here about your nitrous tank, and he really wanted to give it a try. His mom just passed away and he's having a tough time.*

Jimmy had no idea what Leonard was up to—he hadn't heard anything about a *nitrous tank*, whatever that was—but Shirley's expression softened. She looked at Jimmy as if she were seeing him for the first time.

I'm sorry, she said. *That must be hard for you.*

It's okay, Jimmy told her, but then he realized how that sounded and tried again. *I mean, it's not okay, it really sucks, it's just, you know, that's what happened. She had cancer, but . . . it was something with her heart . . . I don't know. She's over at Grandview Cemetery, not too far from the pond . . .*

Jimmy still did that sometimes, just started babbling about his mother, and everybody looked embarrassed when he was done. Shirley sighed and opened the door a little wider.

All right, she said. *But just for a few minutes. And try to keep your voices down, okay?*

- 7 -

The inside of the house wasn't messy, exactly—more just busy, all the furniture covered by brightly colored sheets with psychedelic designs on them, some of which clashed with the fuzzy green carpet in the living room. There were kids' toys piled in one corner, along with one of those exercise rollers—a wheel with handles on it—that was supposed to help flatten your stomach. Denise had given their father one for Christmas, but as far as Jimmy knew his dad had never even tried it.

Jimmy wanted to ask Shirley if she used hers, but she was busy sliding a red birthday balloon onto the nozzle of the nitrous tank. It was slender and torpedo-shaped, a battered metal cylinder that looked like something his father might use for welding.

You sure you want to do this? she asked him.

I don't know, Jimmy said. *What's it like?*

She gave him a reassuring smile. She'd seemed like a hard-ass at McDonald's, but she was a lot less intimidating in her own home, a plump, lightly perspiring woman in terry cloth gym shorts and a matching tank top.

It's just laughing gas, she told him. *It's the exact same thing they give you at the dentist.*

How long does it last?

Just a minute or two. You'll get a nice floaty feeling, like you're an astronaut on a space walk.

She meant that as a selling point, but it didn't have the desired effect, because Jimmy had never understood the appeal of being an astronaut. It didn't seem like such a great adventure, risking your life to travel to a place where you couldn't breathe.

Does it give you a hangover?

Jesus fucking Christ, Leonard snapped. He was lounging on the velour recliner in his too-snug uniform, with his feet up and his hands behind his head. *Stop being such a little pussy.*

Shirley glared at him.

Leonard, she said. *Please don't.*

Don't what? Leonard said, like she was the one being the jerk. *I'm just busting his balls.*

Oh my God, Shirley muttered. *How old are you?*

Old enough, Leonard told her. *Least you thought so last night.*

Well, she said, *I hope you enjoyed it, because it's not gonna happen again.*

Yeah right, Leonard said, like he'd heard that one before.

Hey, Shirley. Eddie was sprawled on a beanbag chair next to a stack of picture books. *Go, Dog. Go!*, one of Jimmy's favorites, was on the top. *If you fire Leonard, can I have his job?*

Why would I do that? Shirley asked. *I'd just be replacing one idiot with another.*

She turned back to Jimmy and smiled wearily, like the two of them were the only sensible people in the room.

Here, she said, reaching for the knob on the tank. *Let me show you.*

Jimmy watched as she inflated the balloon halfway, pinched it shut, and brought it to her lips. She looked a little startled as she sucked the gas into her lungs, and then she closed her eyes and went on her space walk. When she came back, she was blinking dreamily, all the worry erased from her face.

Holy shit. She laughed to herself and then she turned to Jimmy. *You ready?*

I guess, he said.

He must have sounded nervous, because she touched her finger to the bottom of his chin.

It's okay, honey, she said. *I'll be right here if you need me.*

That threw him off a little, because no one ever called him *honey* except his mother. She filled the balloon with laughing gas and brought it to the left-hand corner of his mouth, as far away as she could get from his fat lip on the other side.

Just take a little sip, she whispered.

The gas tasted fruity and it hit him hard. He felt a surge of euphoria, but it was too much. His head got big and his legs went wobbly and the world started to flicker on and off, like strobe lights at the Battle of the Bands.

It didn't last that long, but when he opened his eyes, Shirley was propping him up by the armpits and a toddler was standing in the hallway, a pudgy little guy wearing nothing but a saggy diaper and an expression of bitter surprise.

Mama, he said, and then he flung himself on the floor and began to shriek.

- 8 -

The kid threw quite a tantrum, screaming and writhing and pounding the floor. Jimmy kept waiting for Shirley to do something about it, but she just folded her arms across her chest and watched him with a bored expression, like this was a rerun of a show she'd already seen a hundred times. There were a couple of false endings and a brief case of the hiccups before the kid pulled himself together.

Are you done? Shirley waggled the deflated balloon. *Is this what you want?*

The toddler nodded and staggered into the living room, a rope of snot dangling from one nostril, swaying like a pendulum. He waited patiently while Shirley blew up the balloon, tied it off, and placed it in his outstretched hands. He snatched it to his chest and gazed at Jimmy with a sullen expression.

Mine, he said.

Shirley lifted him off the floor and carried him over to the couch.

He's a sweetie, she said, and kissed the top of his head. *He's just a little under the weather.*

You gonna maybe wipe his nose? Leonard asked. *It's kinda gross.*

There weren't any tissues handy, so Shirley used her fingers to pinch off the snot. The kid just sat there like the baby Jesus in a painting, hugging the red balloon and looking perfectly content.

There's more where that came from, Shirley said, wiping her hand on her shorts. *It's amazing how much disgusting stuff comes out of this cute little body.*

Jimmy's head was still cloudy from the gas, so it took him a moment to fully register the contrast between the mother and the child—Shirley pasty and pink-cheeked, and her son golden brown, like he'd been working hard on his tan, his hair a mop of dirty-blond curls.

What's his name? Jimmy asked.

Antoine, Shirley replied. *Just like his dad.*

Eddie smirked at Leonard.

Wanna hear something funny? he said. *Jimmy thought you might be the father.*

Leonard didn't find this as amusing as Eddie did.

What the fuck? he said. *Do I look like a _______?*

Nothing happened for a second or two. The word just hung in the air like a bad smell, shocking in a way it hadn't been in the car. Shirley rose from the couch as if Antoine were weightless in her arms, and jutted her chin at Leonard.

Get out of my house, she said. Her voice wasn't loud, but there was an edge to it. *I mean it, Leonard. Get the fuck out.*

Leonard cranked the recliner handle and sat up straight.

Take it easy, he said. *I was just—*

What kind of person are you? she asked. *Talking like that in front of my son.*

He's two years old, Leonard said. *He doesn't even know what it means.*

Not yet, Shirley said. *But I'm sure you'll be happy to explain it to him when he's a little older.*

Antoine whimpered in her arms; she joggled him up and down and told him everything was okay. When she turned back to Leonard, there was a big fake smile on her face. Her voice was as bright and cheerful as a kindergarten teacher's.

I think it's time for you nice boys to go, she said. *It's been such a fun visit but my son and I need to get some rest.*

Leonard didn't move, but Eddie extricated himself from the beanbag chair and got to his feet.

Come on, he muttered. *We should probably . . .*

Leonard groaned in frustration, but he got up and followed Eddie. Jimmy was the last to leave. He wanted to apologize to Shirley, or at least say something to let her know that he wasn't a jerk like Leonard, but he didn't know where to start, so he just gave her a half-assed wave as he slipped out the door.

- 9 -

They walked back to the car and got inside. Eddie started the engine, but then they just sat there, taking a moment to regroup. It was mortifying to be thrown out of someone's house—it had never happened to Jimmy before—and all three of them could feel the sting of it. Or at least it seemed that way, until Leonard shook his head and laughed, like something bizarre and unfair had just happened.

I don't know what got into her, he said. *She's not usually such a bitch.*

Eddie said maybe it was that time of the month, but Leonard said no, last week had been that time of the month, so that was no excuse.

She was just in a shitty mood, he said. *I could tell as soon as she answered the door. It wasn't even that late. And then she freaks out about nothing.*

She didn't like the word you said, Jimmy told him.

Leonard gave him a look like, No shit, Sherlock.

I wasn't even talking about the kid, he said. *I was talking about her ex.*

Eddie shifted into gear and made a tight three-point turn, spinning the wheel with the flat of his palm.

Must be weird, he said. *Knowing she's been with a Black guy.*

It's pretty messed up, Leonard agreed.

A gloomy silence filled the car as they drove through the center of South Drumford, passing a small park that had an authentic-looking World War II battle tank sitting next to a playground, its gun aimed right at the monkey bars.

I don't get it, Jimmy said. *What's it matter if the guy's Black or white or whatever? People are just people, right?*

Leonard twisted around in his seat.

Easy for you to say. You're from Creamwood. You don't have to live with 'em.

Jimmy's mind flashed on Hector, lying on the beach towel, but he knew better than to mention it to Leonard.

Yeah, he said, *but it's not fair to generalize, right?*

Generalize? Leonard said. *What the fuck are you talking about?*

You know, it's like when you say something about a whole bunch of—

I know what it means, Leonard said. *Jesus Christ, Eddie, where'd you find this kid?*

Jimmy's okay, Eddie assured him. *He's actually having some girlfriend trouble too.*

Really? Leonard looked surprised. *Jimmy's got a girlfriend?*

Foxy little cheerleader, Eddie said. *But now she's fucking his best friend.*

She is not, Jimmy said. *Why do you keep saying that?*

Your best friend? Leonard was offended on Jimmy's behalf. *Damn. That's cold.*

Tell me about it, Eddie said. *Little douchebag named Cellucci, thinks he's hot shit. Stole Jimmy's girl right after his mother died. And he gave him that fat lip too.*

We were just playing basketball, Jimmy said, but Leonard wasn't listening.

You fucking kidding me? he said. *Where does this asshole live?*

- 10 -

Ten minutes later they were back in Creamwood, parked across from Greg's house on Azalea Road, a quiet street that bordered the wooded section of Lenape Park.

Ring the doorbell, Leonard told him. *And then when he answers, just haul off and punch him in the face. Don't even say hello.*

I'm not gonna do that, Jimmy said.

Why not? Leonard seemed genuinely puzzled. *You're totally within your rights.*

Greg's house was a standard-issue Creamwood split-level, slate gray with a one-car garage. Its only distinguishing feature was a bay window in the front, which Greg's mom was really proud of. She was always changing the decorations on the inside shelf depending on the season. Right now it was a big vase of sunflowers.

What if his mother answers? Jimmy asked.

Bust her in the mouth too, Leonard said. *Serves her right for raising a little douchebag.*

The house was dark, except for a TV flickering in the living room. Jimmy couldn't see who was watching, but he guessed it was Mr.

Cellucci. Most likely he was fast asleep on the couch with his head thrown back, snoring like he was being strangled by a pair of invisible hands. Sometimes he spent the whole night like that and woke up in his rumpled work clothes from the day before.

Let's just go, Jimmy said. *I really don't wanna be here.*

Give it a minute, Leonard told him. *Maybe he'll come walking down the street and all three of us can jump him.*

You could always toss a rock through that big window, Eddie suggested. *That'll get their attention.*

Or a Molotov cocktail, Leonard added.

Azalea wasn't a dead end, but it didn't connect to any major streets. It was eerily silent except for the insects and tree frogs in the park, the dull drone of a summer night. It would have been relaxing to sit there under other circumstances, almost like a camping trip.

I mean it, Jimmy said. *Let's get outta here.*

Eddie and Leonard ignored him, like he hadn't even spoken, and Jimmy wondered later why he didn't just get out of the car and start walking home. He remembered wanting to leave, and reaching for the door handle, but for some reason he couldn't complete the motion—it was almost like something was restraining him, a hand clamped on his shoulder—and then it was too late.

Shhhh. Eddie pressed a finger to his lips. *You hear that?*

The sound was faint at first, a human voice in the distance, and Jimmy thought maybe Greg was singing as he walked, which seemed odd, because Greg wasn't really into music.

Please don't hurt him, he said, or maybe he just thought he said it, but it didn't matter, because it wasn't Greg. Larry Brunner had already emerged from the darkness, rolling his wheelchair down the middle of the empty street, and now the words were loud and clear.

Here I coooome, motherfucker!

He was moving at a surprisingly brisk clip, spinning the wheels with his gloved hands, his leg stumps jutting out in front of him.

Here I come!

Larry was a long-haired guy with a powerful upper body, a linebacker for the Creamwood Chiefs before he went to Vietnam. He was leaning forward in his seat, his arms moving like pistons, and there was an oddly playful note in his voice, like he was chasing someone who wanted to be caught, though his prey was nowhere in sight.

Here I coooome, motherfucker!

The chant faded as he continued down the street and turned the corner onto Evensong Road. Larry was a familiar presence in Creamwood, but not so familiar that there wasn't an instinctive moment of silence in his wake. When it was okay to talk again, Eddie glanced at Jimmy in the rearview mirror.

Hey, he said, like he'd just had a bright idea. *What about your cousin?*

My cousin? Jimmy said.

You know, the draft dodger.

He's not a draft dodger. I don't know why everybody keeps saying that. He had a medical exemption.

Whatever, Eddie said. *The hippie with the flat feet. Is that better?*

What about him?

I was just wondering, Eddie said. *You think he might have some weed?*

- 11 -

Jimmy didn't even have to ask. He got his answer the moment Wayne opened the door, and the house exhaled a skunky cloud of smoke right into his face. It was close to midnight by then, but Wayne seemed happy to see him.

Heyyy, Jimmy. His voice was slow and his eyes were sleepy. *C'mon in, brother.*

Just for a minute. Jimmy nodded at the Vega, which was idling at the curb, issuing a throaty grumble from under the hood. *I'm with some guys.*

Invite 'em in. We're having a little party.

We're kind of in a hurry, Jimmy said. *We were just hoping we could maybe buy a little weed if you have any extra.*

Wayne's dreamy smile disappeared.

I'm not a dealer, man.

No, I know, Jimmy said. *I didn't mean—*

I'm not gonna charge you, Wayne said. *You're my favorite cousin. How much you need?*

I don't know. Maybe just a joint?

I'm outta papers, Wayne said. *I could pack you a bowl, though. Would that be cool?*

That would be excellent.

Wayne opened the door a little wider.

Come on in while I get it. I'm not gonna leave you standing out here like a Jehovah's Witness.

Jimmy didn't know what that was, but it didn't sound great. He gave Leonard and Eddie a quick thumbs-up and ducked inside the house. Wayne paused in the foyer, trying to remember where he'd stashed his spare pipe. He thought it might be in his guitar case, but he wasn't a hundred percent sure about that. If it wasn't there, he said, it was probably down in the laundry room, though there was a slim possibility it was under the couch in the sunporch.

I know it's around here somewhere, he said. *Just gimme a minute to track it down.*

While he went off in search of the pipe, Jimmy poked his head into the living room to say hello. It wasn't much of a party, just Nilda, Hector, and a young Black woman he'd never seen before. It was super mellow in there, "Mercy Mercy Me" playing on the stereo, a red lava lamp painting the room with swirling blobs of color.

Yo, Cousin Jimmy, Hector called out. *What's the word?*

Hey, Hector, Jimmy said. *I'm just, you know . . . borrowing some pot.*

Hector looked amused.

Hear that? he said. *Cousin Jimmy just "borrowing" some pot.*

Like going to the library, Nilda said. *Just make sure you return it in two weeks.*

Gotta get me one of those *library cards,* the younger woman said, and they all laughed.

Cousin Jimmy, Hector said, *this is Yvette. Yvette, this is Cousin Jimmy from next door.*

Yvette and Jimmy said their hellos. She was small and dark-skinned, with a wide, pretty smile. Her hair was straight and parted on the side, though she'd used a curling iron to flip the edges back from her cheeks, like Denise did when she had a date.

You hungry? Nilda asked. *There's some Chinese in the fridge. You like pork fried rice?*

Never had it, Jimmy said. *Is it good?*

Delicious, Yvette told him. *The beef with broccoli is even better, but that's all gone.*

Did I hear you right? Hector asked. *Never had fried rice? How is that possible?*

My father doesn't like Chinese food, Jimmy explained. *He says it's not very filling.*

Nilda chuckled and patted her stomach.

Don't know about that, she said.

You know what? Hector told him. *We're gonna have to take you to the Golden Wok sometime. Best Chinese restaurant in Newark.*

Don't worry, Yvette told him. *We'll show you how to use the chopsticks.*

Wayne wandered into the living room and asked what they were talking about. Hector filled him in on the plan to treat Jimmy to some mind-blowing Szechuan food.

Count me in, Wayne said. *You know I love the Wok.*

Hector thought it over and then he shook his head.

Sorry, he said. *No hippies allowed.*

They all thought that was hilarious, even Wayne. When they were done laughing, he handed Jimmy a pipe with a red stem and a shiny copper bowl that was filled to the brim with the greenest weed Jimmy had ever seen.

It was in my toolbox, Wayne said. *Just like I thought.*

Thanks, Jimmy said. *That's really nice of you.*

It was time to go, but he didn't want to leave. He wanted to stay right there, listening to Marvin Gaye and maybe even trying some of the pork fried rice they'd been talking about. Some part of him thought that if he lingered long enough, Eddie and Leonard would get tired of waiting and drive away, but the clearer part of his brain knew that was a fantasy. If they got impatient enough, they would get out of the car and ring the doorbell, and Wayne would invite them in, and Jimmy had no idea what would happen after that, but he didn't think it would be anything good.

He resented Eddie and Leonard for that, for knowing that they would feel free to barge in and say something mean or stupid or just thoughtless to people they didn't even know, but he was also a little upset with Wayne, because it was one thing when it was just him and Nilda and the neighbors were scratching their heads, and it was a whole other thing now that Hector had joined them, and Yvette was there too. He couldn't tell if Wayne was looking for trouble, or if he'd just been away from Creamwood for too long and had forgotten how it worked.

Eddie honked twice, and Jimmy felt himself flinch.

All right, he said. *Guess I better get going.*

- 12 -

Wayne's weed was amazing, by far the best Jimmy had ever smoked. It wiped away all the bad feelings that had been building up inside of him over the course of the night, and replaced them with a quiet sense of wonder. He let go of the shame he'd felt at Shirley's house, and his growing doubts about Eddie and Leonard—especially Leonard—and the anxiety that had rattled him outside of Greg's house and then again at Wayne and Nilda's. He was happy to be back on the move, cruising through a familiar but subtly altered world, the edges of the buildings a little sharper, the lights a little more glittery, time a little slower.

This is primo shit, Leonard said. *Where'd he get it?*

I don't know. I didn't ask.

He packed that bowl pretty tight, Eddie observed. *He must really like you.*

I'm his favorite cousin, Jimmy said.

Seriously, though, Leonard told him. *You should find out who his connection is.*

They rumbled through the sleepy center of town, past the candy store and the liquor store and Sturmer's Deli. They passed Fineman's Pharmacy, where Jimmy had gone so often to pick up his mother's prescriptions, and Miss Evelyn's Academy of Dance, where Denise had been a star pupil in her younger days, practicing pliés and jetés in her pink leotard. When they got to Poodle Pete's, Jimmy torqued his head to check out the windows on the second floor, but Olivia's apartment was dark. He wondered how the field trip had gone. It would have been nice to sit with her on the bus, their knees and elbows touching, maybe even holding hands, everyone else laughing and singing and goofing around, not giving them a second thought.

Your cousin really have flat feet? Leonard asked. *Or is that just bullshit?*

I don't know, Jimmy said. *I never asked. But I'm glad he didn't go to Vietnam.*

Leonard grunted thoughtfully, like Jimmy had a point.

Eddie's uncle went over there, he said. *Messed him up pretty good.*

It wasn't Vietnam, Eddie said. *He just made a mistake.*

Some mistake, Leonard said. *Ten years to life in Rahway Prison.*

Jimmy looked at Eddie.

Is that true? You have an uncle who went to Rahway?

Eddie seemed surprised by the question.

Thought I told you. He patted the dashboard. *This used to be his car.*

How long's he in for?

Eddie didn't answer right away, and Jimmy got the feeling that he shouldn't have asked.

His uncle's dead, Leonard said. *He hung himself in his cell.*

Holy shit, Jimmy said. *Why did he—?*

You know what? Eddie said. *This is bumming me out. How about we listen to some tunes?*

He turned on the radio, and Van Morrison's voice filled the car, talking about what a fantabulous night it was.

Fucking moondance, Leonard muttered, but he didn't change the station.

Jimmy couldn't help wondering what Eddie's uncle had done to get himself sent to Rahway, because that was where the worst criminals in New Jersey went—the murderers and rapists and armed robbers—but he knew it wasn't the right time to ask.

It must have been weird for Eddie, waking up one morning and learning that he was the proud owner of a dead man's car. It was weird for Jimmy too, because he'd been riding around in that car for the past two months, and had never given a second thought to its previous owner. As far as he could remember, Eddie had mentioned him only once, Jimmy's very first time in the Vega.

Used to be my uncle's, he said. *This thing can fly.*

Jimmy hadn't thought about that night in a while, Eddie stopping for him outside the funeral home, and the way he'd felt climbing into the car, like he didn't really have a choice. He remembered driving past Greg and Janie and his other eighth-grade friends and feeling like a ghost, like he no longer inhabited the same reality as they did, an innocent world of baseball games and ice cream cones and who had a crush on who, and that feeling had only gotten stronger over the course of the summer. And now Eddie was looking at Leonard, tapping his finger on the speedometer.

Jimmy doesn't think it can do a hundred.

They were waiting at a red light when he said this, and Jimmy hadn't been paying attention to where they were, but now he saw the sign, an arrow pointing to the ramp of the Garden State Parkway. Leonard turned and looked at him.

Better buckle up, he said, and he wasn't smiling.

- 13 -

The light changed while Jimmy was searching for the lap belt. Eddie stepped on the gas and accelerated onto the entrance ramp, and they were already moving at highway speed by the time they approached the merge. Jimmy found both ends of the safety belt, but before he could complete the linkage, Eddie hit the brakes and spun the wheel. The Vega fishtailed onto the highway, the back end spinning toward where the front should have been, and Jimmy lost his balance and toppled face down onto the back seat.

It was a strange and disturbing sensation, as if he were falling through a denser, stickier kind of air. It was buzzing in his ear, and he could smell it too, that same sweet and rotten odor he'd noticed before.

He pushed himself up from the seat—he could feel something nasty clinging to his skin and hair like a cobweb—and started swiping at his head, but then he stopped, because Eddie was flooring it and they were heading straight for the oncoming traffic, though there wasn't much of it at that time of night.

Eddie, Jimmy said. *I think you're going the wrong way,* but Eddie wasn't listening, and the car they were about to collide with swerved at the last second, passing so closely that Jimmy could see the shock on the driver's face, and that happened three or four more times, horns blaring, headlights veering miraculously out of their path, until they hit a patch of empty road and Eddie stomped on the brakes and repeated the same maneuver as before, the Vega sliding and spinning and then straightening out, except that this time they were flowing in the same direction as everyone else, and traveling at a legal rate of speed. Eddie even turned on his blinker before they reached the exit, and the ramp deposited them in the exact same place they'd started from.

- 14 -

The terror didn't really hit him until he was home and safe in his bed, and could face the truth of what had happened, just how close he'd come to dying. He lay there in the dark with his eyes wide open, imagining his own wake, the whole town lined up to pay their respects, his father and sister standing by the open coffin, their faces crushed and broken by grief. It would be too much for them, one tragedy piled on top of another, their family divided by two.

All he'd felt in the moment was a kind of stoned amazement, the insanity of driving the wrong way down the highway at a hundred miles an hour, and the exhilaration of getting away with it. He'd been numb after that, too stunned to do anything but hug himself in the back seat, listening to the sound of Eddie's and Leonard's giddy voices, but not the words they were saying.

He breathed a little easier after they dropped Leonard off at his house in South Drumford. It was such a relief to be done with him, to escape from the back seat and take his usual spot up front. Eddie asked if he was okay and Jimmy said he was fine, just a little tired, and they were quiet all the way back to Creamwood.

Something was bugging him, though, a question that had shaken loose on the Parkway, while they were racing toward the oncoming headlights. Jimmy waited as long as he could to ask it, keeping it to himself until they were back on Morgan Street, pulling up at the curb in front of his house.

Eddie, he said. *What was your uncle's name?*

My career as a literary writer lasted about fifteen years. I published three novels and a story collection—a respectable output—but each one of them sold fewer copies than the last, and nobody even wanted to hear my idea for book number five. My editor said the market had changed, and my agent stopped returning my calls.

I made a deal with Molly. We had enough savings to get through another year, and I told her I would use that time to write one last book. I promised her that this one would be commercial—my version of a Stephen King novel—something supernatural and suspenseful that people would actually want to read for fun. If that didn't work, I gave her my word that I would close up shop and go back to teaching English at a prep school.

That was how the original noir version of *Ghost Teacher* was born. The title character was a sad sack named Dave Duckworth, a kindhearted special ed teacher at a public high school run by a depraved, donut-loving principal. Every day Dave goes to work and watches in silent agony as bullies and cruel jocks taunt and humiliate his beloved students. He tries to intervene in chapter two, and suffers a severe beating that leaves him with a black eye and a missing front tooth.

In chapter three, Dave chokes to death on a cafeteria hot dog and discovers, to his profound dismay, that his spirit remains trapped inside the high school where he's been so miserable. He mopes around for a few days, but eventually decides to make the best of a bad situation. He draws up an Enemies List and methodically plots his revenge, taking advantage of his invisibility to arrange a series of grisly "accidents." One bad guy amputates his own hand on a table saw in wood shop; another gets an arrow through the neck during an archery lesson in PE. There's a rogue Zamboni, a Driver's Ed car with faulty brakes, and a poison jelly cruller for the principal.

It wasn't a subtle book, but it was a blast to write. As a literary novelist, I'd worked at a glacial pace, agonizing over metaphors, second-guessing every adverb. Most days I was lucky if I eked out a hundred words. But that first *Ghost Teacher* book just poured out of me—five, six, seven pages in a sitting—the prose simple and direct, the energy flowing freely from my brain to my fingers.

This is how it's supposed to be, I thought. *This is what it feels like to be a writer.*

I found a new agent—a freshly downsized former editor with a chip on her shoulder—and we sent the book out with a feeling of cautious optimism. I believed that I'd found my voice and written something dark and fun and compelling, and I was genuinely shocked when the rejections started dribbling in.

"Exhausting and derivative."

"Monotonous and relentless."

"What happened to the guy who wrote *Orphan Song*?"

I went into a tailspin, a deep, inconsolable funk, probably the worst crisis of my adult life. But a deal was a deal—we had a mortgage to pay and two kids to put through college—so I started writing letters to private schools, pretending to be excited about returning to the classroom and transmitting my love of literature to a new generation. I'd gone on a couple of dispiriting interviews, when I got an unexpected call from my agent.

"Good news," she said. "We have some serious interest from Amy Lesniak at Pennyworth Press."

"Pennyworth? Don't they do kids' books?"

"I went to Barnard with Amy," she continued. "She really loves the concept. But you'd need to brighten it up a little."

"What does that mean? How do you brighten up a horror story?"

"She says they're looking for a more likeable main character, preferably female, and a lot less violence. No amputations or archery accidents. She says the ghost should be a positive role model, more like a guiding spirit."

"That sounds terrible," I said.

"She thinks with the right tweaks it might have series potential."

"That's all well and good," I said. "But I'm not a YA hack."

"I hear you," she said. "But frankly, at this stage of your career . . ."

She was kind enough not to complete the sentence.

In the rewrite, Dave Duckworth turned into Ellen Farkas, a spunky fourth-grade teacher who's already a ghost when the story begins (we never learn how she died). She drifts around the school, helping the kids who are struggling—the shy ones and the clumsy ones, the underdogs and outsiders who need a little boost. She might guide an errant finger to the correct note at a piano recital, or whisper a crucial line into the ear of a petrified first-time actor in the holiday play. Every once in a while, she pushes the ethical envelope a bit, slowing down a boastful runner by tugging on the back of his shirt, allowing a lovable but unathletic kid to win the race for once—that kind of thing, a feel-good thumb on the scales of justice.

The first book did pretty well, and *Ghost Teacher to the Rescue!* did even better. The third installment, *Ghost Teacher Loves You*, was a huge bestseller. When it got optioned for TV, I made sure to attach myself to the project as a screenwriter, and before too long we had moved to LA, where I spent several years of my life producing a show full of happy endings and heartwarming lessons, and earning a lot of money in the process. I know for a fact that some of my old grad school classmates think of me as a sellout, but that makes it sound like I had some kind of cynical plan, when really I was just sliding down a cliff, grabbing for any handhold within reach, and hanging on for dear life when I caught one.

MR. INNOCENT

- 1 -

There was nothing deader than downtown Creamwood on a sweltering Sunday afternoon in the middle of August. The stores were closed and the sidewalks were deserted, except for the rusty garbage cans lining the curb, their contents baking in the sun. You could almost see the stench rising up through the lids, like squiggly lines in a cartoon.

Jimmy stopped in front of Poodle Pete's and pretended to examine the window display, which featured a photo gallery of snooty-looking dogs with shaved bodies and fluffy heads, one more hideous than the next. When he was sure no one was looking, he ducked into the side door that led up to Olivia's apartment. He rang the bell in the vestibule, waited a few seconds, and then rang it again, this time pressing harder.

He'd been trying to find her all weekend. She wasn't staying at the Randowskis'—he'd gone over there several times to check—and no one was answering her home phone. He rang the bell a third time just to be sure, and then headed up a dim flight of stairs that reeked of cat food and insecticide. Kneeling on a prickly welcome mat, he slipped an envelope under the door of apartment 2B. It had Olivia's name on the front and a brief note tucked inside.

Call me as soon as you can. I think I know who Uncle Bob is.

He was still on his knees when the door swung open and he found himself staring at a woman's feet. His startled gaze traveled up the length of her veiny legs to the hem of a short pink nightie.

I thought you were the postman, Mrs. Riley said. *But he only rings twice.*

Jimmy scrambled to his feet, his face warming with embarrassment. The front of her nightie had some frilly ruffles, so it wasn't completely see-through, but it was flimsy enough that he didn't know where to look.

Sorry, he said. *I didn't mean to wake you.*

I wasn't sleeping. She reached up with both hands and made some quick adjustments to her hair, which was flatter on one side than the other. *Just resting in front of the fan. Nothing else to do in this heat.*

It's pretty bad, Jimmy agreed. *It's supposed to get a little better tomorrow.*

Thanks for the weather report. She looked down at the envelope and nudged it with her toe. *Is that for me?*

It's for Olivia. I've been trying to—

Too bad. She clucked her tongue with disappointment. *I thought I had a secret admirer.*

Jimmy knew she was joking, but wasn't sure if he was supposed to laugh. Before he could decide, she bent down to retrieve the envelope. He didn't avert his eyes quickly enough and saw right down the front of her nightie.

That's so sweet, she said once she'd straightened up. *Olivia Jean's first love letter.*

It's not a love letter, Jimmy told her.

Sure, honey. She gave him a wink, like they had a private understanding. *Whatever you say.*

- 2 -

You had to walk or bike down the main path in Lenape Park for a minute or two, going past the tennis courts and the softball field, before you got to the picnic pavilion that was the main gathering place for Summer Rec. The only other building in the vicinity was the equipment shed, which also housed the restrooms.

Jimmy arrived early on Monday morning and found Olivia waiting by the shed, sitting with her back to the cinder block wall, her long legs stretched in front of her. No one else was around.

I can't believe you came to my apartment, she said.

She was a little more dressed up than usual, in a blue-and-white batik skirt and the same leotard top she'd worn the night they did the Ouija board, the black one with Saturn on the front.

I couldn't find you, he said. *I didn't know what else to do.*

I was in Lavallette with Peg. I would've told you on the bus, but you forgot your permission slip, remember?

That wasn't my fault. Nobody told me I needed one.

She patted the ground, inviting him to join her. He lowered himself onto the cool concrete apron that surrounded the shed.

I hope your mom wasn't too upset. I think I woke her from—

Upset? Olivia thought that was pretty funny. *She's thrilled. She keeps calling you "my cute little boyfriend," like it's the greatest thing that ever happened.*

Jimmy didn't like the sound of that phrase—*cute little boyfriend*—especially when they were sitting so close together, and you could see how much longer her legs were than his. As if she could read his mind, Olivia drew her knees up and hugged them to her chest.

Didn't you ever have a boyfriend before? he asked.

She scrunched up her face, like that was a tough question.

I never liked anybody enough, she said. *And nobody ever liked me.*

They were quiet after that, and then she reached for his hand, threading her fingers through his. They kept their eyes straight ahead, as if their hands needed a little privacy.

You don't have to believe it, she said, *but I knew you were looking for me. The whole weekend, I had this really strong feeling that there was something you wanted to tell me.*

Really? He traced the hard part of her thumb with the soft part of his own. *That's pretty weird.*

We're on the same wavelength, she told him. *I've been feeling it all summer.*

He turned to look at her. She had a new hairdo—two thin braids circled her head like a crown—and she was wearing eye makeup too, which made her look older than usual, more like the college student she was about to become.

I like the braids, he said.

She leaned closer. He thought she was going to kiss him, but she just touched her forehead to his and left it there, as if she was too tired to do anything else. They stayed like that for a while, breathing in unison, until they were startled by the ratchety sound of the shed door being yanked up. They turned to see Doug squinting at them from around the side of the building, wearing a bright white baseball cap with a Greek letter on the front.

Happy Monday, he said, trying to sound casual, like there was nothing unusual about the sight of two of his counselors holding hands. *Gonna be another scorcher.*

- 3 -

Jimmy stuck close to the crafts table that morning. The kids were making ashtrays, gluing small ceramic tiles into metal containers that looked like soap dishes. Once they got started, they didn't need much guidance, so he was finally able to tell Olivia about Eddie's uncle.

His name was Bobby Eberhart. He died in Rahway Prison.

Eddie had told him the whole story on Saturday night, while they were parked in front of Jimmy's house.

I think I heard something about that at school, she said, pressing a tile into an ashtray she was making for her mother. It had an intricate design, a star inside a circle. *Didn't he kill his wife or something?*

Fiancée, Jimmy told her. His own ashtray was simple compared to hers—just an alternating pattern of green and yellow—but he was happy with the way it was shaping up. *He caught her in bed with another guy and I guess he just lost it. And then he felt really bad about what he'd done, and that's why he hung himself.*

That's a depressing story. She pondered her mosaic like it was a chessboard. *Kinda stupid, though. He could've just broken up with her and gone on with his life. Would've saved everyone a lot of grief.*

Jimmy had said something similar to Eddie, and it hadn't gone over very well.

Come on, Eddie said. *What was he supposed to do? She's fucking this other guy and she didn't even take off her engagement ring. I mean, yeah, he shouldn't have killed her, but . . .*

Olivia deposited some glue onto her tray, a single perfect drop.

So you really think it's him? The same Uncle Bob?

I think so. I've been riding around in his car the whole summer. I guess that's how he knows me.

He didn't tell her that he'd sometimes sensed a ghostly presence in the back seat of the Vega. He'd assumed it was his mother, watching over him, but it turned out to be a man who'd killed a woman with his bare hands, a woman he supposedly loved. It made him sick just thinking about it.

Do you want to talk to him? she asked. *We can try the Ouija board again.*

No, Jimmy said. *I don't want to talk to him. I don't even want to think about him. It really creeps me out.*

Olivia reached into the bowl of loose tiles and selected a red one. Then she changed her mind and went for a blue one instead.

I get that, she said. *I just wish we hadn't asked him to find your mother.*

- 4 -

She kissed him in the equipment shed at the end of the day—just once, very quickly—and then she pressed her lips to his ear.

I want to be alone with you, she said. *Before I leave for college. There's something I want to—*

She must have heard footsteps, because she whirled away from him a second before Nick and Heather entered the shed, their arms full of board games and athletic gear. Doug followed a moment later, carrying dismantled sections of the tetherball pole, and everybody started talking and goofing around, and he never got to hear the rest of whatever it was she was about to tell him.

He was still high from the kiss, though, biking home from the park, holding on with one hand—he had his green-and-yellow ashtray in the other—as he coasted down East Street under a hazy sky, gliding past the familiar houses, little kids squealing as they ran through a sprinkler, a Mister Softee truck jingling in the distance. It was beautiful but a little unreal, almost like he was pedaling through a good memory, a summer that had already come and gone.

- 5 -

Hector answered the door at Wayne's house.

Cousin Jimmy, he said. *Always a pleasure.*

Hey, Hector. Is Wayne around?

Nah, he's out. Won't be back for a few hours.

What about Nilda?

Her too, Hector said. *No one here but me and the TV. You wanna come in?*

No thanks. I just wanted to return this. He held up Wayne's pipe, along with his new ashtray. *And I have a little gift too. You know, just to say thanks.*

Hector opened the screen door. He was wearing a pair of baggy swim trunks and a tie-dyed T-shirt that must have belonged to Wayne.

It's hot out there, he said. *Come on in and have something cool to drink.*

Jimmy followed him into the kitchen and took a seat while Hector got a couple of glasses from the cabinet.

You like Gatorade? he asked.

Never tried it, Jimmy said. *My father thinks it's a gimmick.*

Your dad's got a lot of opinions, huh?

Hector poured their drinks, added some crushed ice from the dispenser on the refrigerator door, and joined Jimmy at the table.

This shit is full of salt, he said, *but there's so much sugar you can't even taste it.*

Why would they do that? Jimmy asked. *Nobody wants a salty drink.*

You think you don't, Hector said. *But really you do. There's a science to it. Your body needs the sodium.*

Jimmy took a cautious sip and grunted his approval. Hector pointed at Jimmy's T-shirt.

Counselor, he said. *Good for you.*

I'm not a real one, Jimmy told him. *They just gave me the shirt because they feel sorry for me. You know, because my mother died.*

That's a hard thing, Jimmy. I'm sorry.

Yeah, Jimmy said. *She was a good mom.*

They were quiet for a bit. Jimmy examined the fruit bowl on the table, three plums and a single bruised peach.

I lost my mom too, Hector said. *I was nine years old.*

Jesus, Jimmy said. *You were just a kid.*

Long time ago. Hector shrugged, like it was all in the past. *My aunt took me in and raised me. Nilda's mom. Nilda's like a big sister to me.*

She's really cool, Jimmy said.

Nilda? Hector tilted his glass and finished off the dregs of his Gatorade. *Nilda's all right. I'm not sure about that hippie she's married to, but . . .*

Jimmy wasn't sure if he was joking, so he just gave a vague nod. After a second or two, Hector broke into a grin.

I'm just playing, he said. *Wayne's good people. Give you the ugly shirt right off his back.*

- 6 -

Before Jimmy left, Hector opened a container on the counter and pulled out a baggie full of bright green weed.

Nilda and Yvette think I smoke too much, he said as he jammed a big bud into the bowl of Wayne's pipe. *But what am I supposed to do? People leave their grass in a cookie jar?*

Hector took the first hit to get it burning right, then extended his arm toward Jimmy. There was something solemn about the gesture, almost ceremonial. Jimmy took a big puff and then nodded like a connoisseur.

That's really smooth, he said.

High quality, Hector agreed. *Some dude Wayne knows grows it on a farm. That's why it smells so fresh.*

Jimmy felt the rush after his second toke, his body growing lighter, the skin on his face relaxing. Hector reached for the green-and-yellow ashtray and held it up to the light.

Nice work, he said. *You make it yourself?*

Yeah. Just this morning. But you have to be careful with it. The grout's a little moist. It needs to harden overnight.

Hector was taking a hit from the pipe. His eyes got big and then he started to cough, and then the coughing turned into a fit of the giggles.

What'd you . . . just say? he asked, the smoke escaping his mouth in little clouds. *About the grout?*

I said the grout needs to . . .

Jimmy couldn't finish the sentence, because Hector's laughter was contagious, and *grout* was a funnier word than he'd realized.

My son, Hector said, as if quoting an old proverb. *You cannot rush the grout.*

Exactly, Jimmy said. *The grout is like a fine wine.*

Damn right, Hector said. *Respect the fucking grout.*

It's not even that funny, Jimmy pointed out, but they kept on laughing.

All right, enough of that. Hector called for a time-out. *Just don't say that word anymore and I'll be fine.*

Jimmy tapped his finger on the ashtray.

Just needs to harden a little, he said, and then they both started cracking up all over again.

- 7 -

He wasn't in Wayne's house for very long, but it was a whole different day when he came out. The sky had turned slate gray, and the dead air had come alive. A fresh breeze gusted through the trees that lined Morgan Street, flipping the leaves upside down. You could smell the storm coming, and feel the temperature dropping in real time.

Jimmy was standing on the lawn, remembering how he and his mother used to sit on the front stoop sharing an umbrella and watching the rain, when Greg Cellucci came riding down the street on his Raleigh ten-speed and turned in to the driveway. For a second or two, Jimmy thought that maybe he wanted to be friends again, but then he saw the pissed-off look on Greg's face.

What's up? Jimmy asked.

Greg made a huffing noise. *Like you don't know.*

He dropped his bike on the ground and walked toward Jimmy, his hands clenching into fists.

Greg, Jimmy said. *I don't want to fight you.*

Greg just kept coming. When he was close enough to throw a

punch, he knelt down in the grass and kissed the tops of Jimmy's dirty white sneakers, first the right one and then the left.

What are you doing? Jimmy asked.

Greg looked up and stared at Jimmy like he hated his guts. And then he started talking in a stilted voice, like a bad actor in a school play.

I, Greg Cellucci, am a piece of shit. I'm a terrible friend and a low-life douchebag. You have every right to spit in my face and kick my teeth in.

Greg stood up and brushed the dead grass off his knees.

There, he said. *You happy now? You feel like a big man?*

No, Jimmy said. *I don't even know what this is about.*

Oh, listen to Mr. Innocent. Greg spat on the ground. *Just tell your psycho friends I apologized, okay? Tell 'em I said every word.*

They're not my friends, Jimmy protested.

Fuck you, Greg told him. *You're such a liar.*

Jimmy wondered how it had happened, if Eddie and Leonard had rung the Celluccis' doorbell, or if they'd just parked on Azalea again and waited for Greg to leave the house, or caught him walking home alone in the dark.

I swear to God, he said. *I never asked them to do that.*

Greg laughed, like he didn't believe a word Jimmy was saying.

Tell 'em they better leave me alone or I'm gonna call the cops. I mean it. My dad knows the chief.

Blushing furiously, Greg walked back to his bike, picked it up, and threw his leg over the crossbar.

What the hell happened to you? he asked.

Jimmy just shrugged, because he didn't even know where to start, and then Greg pedaled off as the rain began to fall, big fat drops that splatted on the ground and left dark blotches where they landed. He stood out there until he was soaked to the skin, and then he went inside and took a shower.

BAD AIR

- 1 -

Summer was winding down, and Jimmy didn't know what to do with himself at night. The only person he wanted to see was Olivia, and she wasn't available. Peg Randowski had returned from the shore to work at a field hockey clinic, and the two of them were spending every possible moment together, because they were best friends and would be leaving for separate colleges right after Labor Day.

Just be patient, Olivia told him. *Peg's going back on Saturday and then we'll have the house to ourselves.*

He had the opposite problem with Eddie, who was always around and was impossible to avoid. Jimmy went out for a walk on Monday night and barely made it a block before the Vega pulled up beside him.

Come on, Eddie said. *Get in the car.*

No thanks, Jimmy told him.

He kept walking and the Vega kept rolling along beside him.

What's the matter? Eddie called out. *You don't like me anymore?*

It's not that, Jimmy said. *I'm just trying to get some exercise.*

Eddie stomped on the brakes. The car rocked back and forth on its chassis.

Don't be such a dick, he said. *I need to talk to you for a second.*

Jimmy stepped into the street and cautiously approached the passenger side window. Eddie was leaning over the gearshift, gazing up at him with a wounded expression.

What's your problem? he asked. *Why are you acting like this?*

It was such an insane question, Jimmy didn't know where to start.

Because you almost killed me, he wanted to say.

Because you scared my friend to death.

Because I can't stand Leonard and don't ever want to see him again.

Because I'm pretty sure there's a ghost in your car.

Listen, Eddie said. *I know it got a little weird the other night. I'm sorry if I scared you.*

Jimmy glanced into the back seat. It looked empty, but he could sense something lurking in the shadows, a sullen, watchful presence, or at least he thought he could. He stepped back from the window.

It's not about that, he said. *It's just . . . I can't ride around with you anymore. I'm not allowed.*

What are you talking about? Eddie said. *Who says you're not allowed?*

My father. He heard I was driving around with an older kid and he got really mad. He doesn't like teenage drivers. He says they think they're immortal.

Eddie looked offended, like Jimmy was speaking in a foreign language.

Come on, he said. *Just get in. I got some weed.*

I told you. Jimmy's voice was firmer now. *My dad won't let me.*

Fuck your dad, Eddie said. *He doesn't give a shit about you.*

What about your dad? Jimmy shot back. *Do you even have one? All I ever heard about was your stupid uncle who killed himself.*

He regretted the words as soon as they were out of his mouth.

Don't talk about my uncle, Eddie said.

Sorry. Jimmy took another small step toward the curb. *I shouldn't have said that.*

He turned and started moving down the sidewalk at a fast clip, like there was someplace he needed to be. He kept waiting for Eddie to chase him down, but the Vega just sat there, almost like it was stunned and wasn't sure what to do next.

- 2 -

It wasn't true about not being allowed in Eddie's car, but it was an easy lie to tell, a way of connecting to a better version of his father than the one he and Denise had been living with that summer—the sad, bleary-eyed guy with nothing to say, the one who couldn't wait to get out of the house and away from his kids, away from the memories he didn't know how to live with.

To his credit, he knew he was screwing up, and occasionally felt bad about it. Every once in a while he'd look at Jimmy from across the kitchen table and say that they should go to a Yankees game one of these days, maybe a Sunday doubleheader, and Jimmy would say that sounded great, though he knew it would never happen. Once a week or so they would literally bump into each other in the hallway outside the bathroom, and his dad would stop and ask how he was doing, and Jimmy would shrug and say he was okay, and then his father would stand there for a few seconds, looking stumped, like there was something else he'd been meaning to say, maybe even something important, but he couldn't remember what it was. And then he'd nod and say, *Okay, then*, and pat Jimmy on the arm, and they'd go their separate ways.

They went out for ice cream exactly one time that summer, just the two of them at Frosty Freez, on a warm evening in early August. They ordered identical hot fudge sundaes—no maraschino cherries, which his father detested—and ate them while sitting on the hood of their Malibu station wagon. His father reminisced about his first date with Jimmy's mom, how they'd gone to a Dairy Queen and shared a banana split, even though he hated bananas.

You should've told her, Jimmy said.

Oh, I told her. But she had her heart set on a banana split, so . . .

He trailed off, like maybe he'd said too much, and that was the end of the story. They finished their sundaes and got back in the car. His father started the engine, but paused with his hand on the gearshift.

I tried to make her happy, he said.

She was, Jimmy told him. *I mean, before . . .*

His father gave that some thought, and then he made a doubtful sound in his throat, like maybe she was and maybe she wasn't.

She loved you and your sister, he said. *That's one thing I know for sure.*

When they got home, his father unearthed a chunky photo album from the bottom of the stereo cabinet and showed Jimmy some of his favorite pictures. He lingered on an image of Jimmy's mom in a 1950s bathing suit, a strapless one-piece that went down to the middle of her thighs. It was a windy day and she was leaning against a curved metal railing that faced the ocean—it was hard to tell if she was standing on a boat or a boardwalk—and gazing back at the camera. His father tapped a finger on the photo, hard enough to leave a smudge on the plastic overlay.

I had no business being with a girl that pretty. She had a nice figure too. Really nice figure.

That gave Jimmy pause, because he'd never thought about his mother's *figure* before. His dad was right, though. She was slender and shapely, a lot like Denise, but she didn't look like she was stuck-up about it.

A lot of guys were after her, his dad said. *I still don't know what she saw in me.*

The album was all snapshots—candid, sometimes blurry photos arranged in rough chronological order—until the very last page, which featured a professional eight-by-ten portrait of Jimmy's mother on her wedding day, a single riveting image that filled all the available space.

She was posed on a stool in her satiny, not-quite-long-sleeved gown, her face turned warily toward the camera. She was trying to smile, but her eyes looked troubled. Jimmy's parents had an official wedding album up in their bedroom, a celebration of the happy couple on their big day—cutting the cake, dancing cheek to cheek, drinking champagne with their arms interlocked at the elbows—but for some reason, this was the photo they'd enlarged and pasted into the family album: the one where she was all alone, a bride without a groom, maybe having some second thoughts before she walked down the aisle.

I told her she was beautiful, his father said, *but she never believed me. She always thought her nose was too big.*

Jimmy nodded, because his mother had often complained about her nose. She used to say that he and Denise were lucky, because they'd gotten Perrini noses from their father, and not Licursi noses from her side of the family. But there was nothing wrong with her face that Jimmy could see.

I mean, look at her, his father said. *Just look at her.*

That was what they did. They sat together on the couch and looked at her.

- 3 -

It was the last week of Rec. A lot of families were on vacation, which was a good thing, because the art supplies were pretty much exhausted. On the final Thursday morning, Olivia brought out a bucket of colored pencil stubs and a stack of construction paper, and told the handful of kids who'd shown up to just go ahead and draw whatever they wanted.

It was a beautiful morning and no one complained. The crafts table was shaded by the pavilion roof, and Heather was playing WABC on her portable radio—"Kung Fu Fighting" and "Rock the Boat" and "When Will I See You Again," the inescapable songs of the summer—and everybody just grabbed a few pencils and went to work, Jimmy and Olivia included.

She kept glancing at him as she drew, and he kept meeting her eyes from across the picnic table. They hadn't kissed since that one time in the shed on Monday, but she'd been flirting with him all week, whispering compliments into his ear, and pressing her leg against his under the table. She'd even tucked a folded note into the front pocket of his shorts at the end of the day on Tuesday.

I've succumbed to your charms, it read.

That was the whole note, one totally ridiculous, deeply arousing sentence, on an otherwise blank sheet of notebook paper. Jimmy had made a few stabs at writing back, but everything he came up with seemed kind of lame—*I like your freckles and long legs*—or way too boring—*Looking forward to Saturday!*—so he just kept crumpling them up and tossing them into the garbage.

Hey, Jimmy, she whispered. *I dreamed about you last night.*

Oh, he said. *What was I doing?*

She leaned a little closer. The kids were all scribbling away, oblivious to their conversation.

That's the weird thing, she said. *I can't remember. I was sleeping over at Peg's, and when I got up this morning she gave me a funny look and said,* Who's Jimmy? *I pretended like I didn't know what she was talking about, and she said that I'd woken up in a panic in the middle of the night. She said I grabbed her arm and kept asking,* Where's Jimmy? What happened to Jimmy? Where did Jimmy go? *She said I was so upset, she actually had to pry my fingers off her wrist.*

That's pretty weird, he said. It was disappointing too, not the kind of dream he'd been hoping for.

I didn't believe her at first, Olivia said. *But then she showed me her wrist and you could see the marks where my fingers had been.*

You must have screamed pretty loud. Isn't Peg's room all the way down the hall?

Yeah, but we were in her parents' bed. We do that sometimes. We get under the covers and talk until one of us dozes off. It's really nice. You know, unless someone's having a nightmare. She laughed softly, but then her face turned serious. *I was so relieved when I saw you this morning. I mean, I know it was just a dream, but . . . I'm really glad you're okay.*

Jimmy was touched by her concern, but also a little distracted by the idea of her and Peg sleeping in the same bed, because everyone thought Peg liked girls, even Janie.

I'm fine, he told her.

She nodded and returned to her drawing, a multicolored hodgepodge of paisleys and comets and amoebas.

If you want, she said, *we could have a sleepover on Saturday. You know, if you don't mind sharing a bed.*

Sleepover? Jimmy said. *You mean . . . with you?*

Uh . . . yeah, she said. *Janie's not gonna be there, if that's what you were hoping.*

I wasn't hoping that.

She studied him for a few seconds, like she wasn't sure if she believed him, and then she reached across the table and drew a random pink squiggle on the top of his drawing, almost like she was signing an autograph.

Just bring your own toothbrush, she said. *Don't even think about using mine.*

- 4 -

He'd spotted the Vega a few times since Monday, but Eddie had just driven by without stopping or slowing down, as if Jimmy was dead to him. It was awkward and a little sad, but Jimmy knew it was for the best. He didn't hate Eddie or anything, but he was glad that they both understood that their summer friendship—or whatever it was—had come to an end.

That was why he was so surprised on Thursday night when Eddie pulled up beside him on a dark stretch of Hollyhock Avenue. Leonard was sitting in the passenger seat in his McDonald's uniform, eating french fries from a bag.

Jimmy, he said, in a fake cheerful voice. *We've been looking all over for you. Where the hell have you been?*

Just wandering around, Jimmy told him.

Leonard made a face, like that was a pathetic thing to be doing.

Get over here, he said. *I want to talk to you.*

What about?

Don't be a little prick, Leonard said. *Get your ass over here.*

Jimmy took a couple of reluctant steps toward the car. When he got within striking distance, Leonard flicked a french fry at his face. It bounced off Jimmy's forehead and landed in the street.

Nice, he said. *Very funny.*

Leonard nodded curtly and flicked another fry. This one caught Jimmy on the cheek and stung a little more than the first one had. He craned his neck, hoping for a little help from Eddie, but Eddie wouldn't even look at him. He just kept staring dead ahead through the windshield, like he was watching a movie at the drive-in. Leonard reached into the bag, pulled out another fry, and popped it into his mouth.

Aren't you gonna thank us? he said.

For what? Jimmy asked.

Leonard laughed, like that was a good try.

For our little chat with Cellucci, he said. *You got your apology, right?*

You scared the shit out of him, Leonard. I never asked you to do that.

Leonard flicked another french fry. Jimmy ducked out of the way and found himself peering into the empty back seat.

Except it wasn't empty.

He could see it now, the thing that must have been there all along. It wasn't much to look at—not even a cloud, just a glitch in the air, like some part of it had gone missing and been replaced by an inferior material, a frayed patch that almost blended in, but not quite.

You should've done it yourself, Leonard said. He glanced over his shoulder to see what Jimmy was staring at, but he didn't notice anything of interest. *Somebody hits you, you gotta hit 'em back. That's the golden rule.*

Jimmy straightened up very slowly, his gaze still fixed on the bad air. It was moving a little, like the quivery lines of static on a TV screen.

Okay, sure. He nodded to Leonard and backed away from the car. *Thanks for the advice.*

He turned and started down the sidewalk, trying to put as much distance between himself and the Vega as possible. He thought about breaking into a run, but he had a feeling it would make things worse. After a brief hesitation, the car lurched into motion and caught up with him.

Hold on, Leonard said. *One more thing.*

Jimmy peered into the back seat. He couldn't see anything from this distance—it was too low, hidden beneath his sightline—but he knew it was there. He could feel it in his stomach, a cold knot, like he'd made a terrible mistake that couldn't be undone.

What the fuck are you looking at? Leonard asked.

Nothing, Jimmy said. *What do you want?*

Leonard popped another fry into his mouth.

I was just wondering why you didn't tell us, he said.

Tell you what?

Jesus Christ. Leonard sighed, like Jimmy was a real pain in the ass. *Why didn't you tell us about your new neighbor?*

I did, Jimmy said. *I told you about my cousin.*

The patch must have been levitating, because he could see it again, a slight disturbance at the bottom of the window frame.

I'm not talking about your cousin, Leonard said. *I'm talking about the new guy.*

Jimmy froze. It was higher now, near the middle of the window, and a little more agitated than before.

How long's he been living there? Leonard asked.

He doesn't live there. It took an effort of will for Jimmy to shift his gaze to the front seat. *He's just visiting.*

Leonard made a face, like he was Columbo and something interesting had just popped into his mind.

Are you sure about that? Because I rang the doorbell and your new neighbor answered, like he was the man of the house.

Why did you ring the bell?

I wanted to see if I could buy a little weed, but he said he didn't have any. I'll tell you what, though, he looked pretty high to me, so he either smoked it or he was lying right to my face.

Jimmy glanced back at the rear window, but all he saw was his own reflection.

He doesn't live there, he said again.

You better hope not, Leonard told him. *Or you can kiss your property values goodbye.*

He shook his head, like that would be a real shame, and then he nodded to Eddie and the Vega pulled away.

- 5 -

Jimmy wasn't sure how they ended up at the Jade Palace instead of the Golden Wok for his inaugural Chinese meal. Maybe just because it was closer, right across the Creamwood border in West Bridgefield, and nobody felt like driving all the way to Newark at rush hour. Whatever the reason, Hector, Nilda, and Yvette were the only Black people in the restaurant.

Jimmy had never been part of a racially mixed group before—not out in public—and he felt extremely self-conscious about it, almost like he and his companions were up on a stage with a spotlight shining on their table. Heads kept swiveling in their direction and then quickly swiveling back, and he could have sworn that everyone in the restaurant was whispering about them, trying to figure out who they were and how they were connected to one another, even though he couldn't hear a word they were saying. It was a relief when the food started to arrive, and he had something else to focus on.

I don't know why they call it an egg roll, Hector said. *No egg in it as far as I can see.*

I'll cut it in half, Yvette told Jimmy. *No big deal if you don't like it.*

Try it with some hot mustard, Wayne said with a smirk. *That'll clear your sinuses.*

I'd skip the mustard if I were you, Nilda advised. *That's the advanced class.*

Jimmy inspected his portion of the egg roll—the filling looked like sauerkraut flecked with mysterious pink bits—and gave it a tentative sniff.

Smells pretty good, he said.

He gathered his courage and took a bite. The shell was greasier than he'd expected, but not in a bad way, and the filling was delicious.

I like it, he told them.

Wait'll you try a wonton, Hector said.

While they waited for their entrees, Yvette told them about her job at the DMV. It was endless paperwork and a daily parade of grumpy citizens, but she liked it okay.

Steady government job, she said. *Do my nine-to-five in the air-conditioning and then I go home.*

That's the spirit, Wayne told her. *Just keep that up for another forty-five years and you'll be golden.*

Nilda glared at him.

Listen to yourself, she said. *Not everybody gets to live rent-free in their daddy's extra house.*

Wayne's beard was so thick it was sometimes hard to read his expressions, but Jimmy caught the flash of irritation in his eyes.

It's just for now, he said. *And we don't have to live there if you hate it so much. Find somewhere else we can afford and I'll be happy to move. Just say the word.*

Nilda sighed very softly and poured herself some jasmine tea from the pot on the table.

I'm not saying I want to move. I'm just saying, most people need to work for a living. Not everybody has the cushion that you do . . . that we do.

I agree, Wayne said. *The whole system's fucked. That's all I was trying to say. I didn't mean—*

It's okay, Yvette told him. *I knew what you meant. And besides, not everybody has to work for a living. Just ask Hector.*

She said this like it was all in fun, but Hector didn't take it that way.

I'm looking, he said. *It's just hard out there if you don't have the connections.*

Not that *hard,* Yvette told him. *And you don't even use the connections that you have.*

Yvette glanced at Wayne, almost like she was asking for permission, and then Wayne nodded at Hector, and Hector looked at Jimmy.

Your dad's a welder, right? He's in the union?

Yeah, Jimmy said. *You have to be. Otherwise they won't hire you.*

Hector nodded, like he knew all about the hiring policy.

You think he'd be my sponsor? he asked.

Your sponsor? Jimmy said. *For what?*

You know, to get into the union. Be an apprentice. You need a member of the local to vouch for you. You think he'd do that for me?

I'm gonna ask him myself, Wayne said. *But if you could put in a good word for Hector, I bet that would help a lot.*

They were all watching Jimmy, waiting for his answer. Jimmy was about to say that it couldn't hurt to try when a hand clamped down on his shoulder.

- 6 -

The hand belonged to Mr. Kazmierski. He was wearing a tweed blazer that Jimmy recognized from school—it was tan with brown patches on the elbows, way too hot for August—and his hugely pregnant wife was standing behind him, both hands cupped beneath her belly, like she was carrying a grocery bag.

Jimmy, he said. *Does your father know you're here?*

Jimmy didn't answer right away, partly because he wasn't sure—he'd left a note under the sugar bowl, but didn't know if his father had seen it—but mainly because Mr. Kazmierski was the last person he wanted to talk to at that particular moment.

I didn't think so. Kaz shifted his gaze to Wayne. *Because I'm pretty sure he wouldn't be too thrilled to see you out in public with Jane Fonda over here. I hope your flat feet aren't giving you too much trouble, Jane.*

Jane Fonda? Wayne squinted at Kaz in disbelief. *Is that supposed to be funny?*

Not really, Kaz replied. *And it wasn't very funny when my brother came home in a box, either.*

Mrs. Kazmierski tugged on her husband's sleeve.

Arthur, she said. *This isn't—*

Kaz yanked his arm free and turned back to Jimmy.

And I don't think your mother would be too happy about it, either. It would break her heart to see you here with these . . . He scanned the table with a frustrated expression, like he couldn't find the word he was looking for. He gestured vaguely at the table. *With these . . . people.*

Damn, said Hector. *Who's this rude motherfucker?*

He's my teacher, Jimmy said, but no one was listening. They were all staring at Kaz, and Kaz was staring at Hector.

You better watch your language, son. There's a lady present.

Son? Hector bristled at the word. *I'm not your son.*

Arthur, Mrs. Kazmierski muttered. *Please.*

You just mind your manners, Kaz told Hector.

Nilda waved her hand to get Kaz's attention.

Excuse me, she said, *but that's not how it works.*

Kaz was annoyed by the interruption.

How what works?

You're the interloper, Nilda told him, like it was the most obvious fact in the world. *You don't get to be offended.*

Interloper? Kaz frowned, like he was unfamiliar with the word.

Yeah, Nilda said. *The person who doesn't belong.*

I'm not the interloper, Kaz said.

Sure you are. We were sitting here, minding our own business, and you barged into our conversation in a very obnoxious way. That makes you the interloper. Check the dictionary if you don't believe me.

That's not the point, Kaz said, but he sounded a little less confident than before. He nodded at Hector. *I was objecting to this one's foul language. I won't tolerate profanity like that in front of my wife.*

Mrs. Kazmierski tugged on his sleeve again, this time a little harder.

Enough, Arthur.

I'm not done, he told her

Mrs. Kazmierski looked mortified.

I beg your pardon, she said. *We had no right to disturb your meal.*

She shot a disgusted glance at her husband and then she lumbered away, moving carefully through the maze of tables, still supporting her belly with both hands. Kaz watched her for a moment, and then he turned back to Nilda.

Interloper, he said, and then he shook his head. *That's pretty funny coming from you.*

Two waiters arrived with more food just as Kaz set off in pursuit of his wife. He caught up to her near the front door, and they had a tense exchange of words before heading outside.

I don't go for that "son" shit, Hector said, and Jimmy could see how upset he was. *Don't take that tone with me.*

Let it go, Yvette told him. *Let's just enjoy our dinner.*

Pass the rice, Wayne said. *Hanoi Jane's got the munchies.*

The food was good and plentiful, and Jimmy liked it all, especially the beef with broccoli. The fortune cookies were the only disappointment. The cookies were a little stale, and the fortunes turned out to be way off base, as clueless about the future as the people who cracked them open.

WILD WORLD

- 1 -

Denise was away that weekend, canoeing on the Delaware River with a group of her high school friends, so Jimmy was alone in the kitchen when his father got home from work on Saturday evening, sweaty and tired after a full day of double overtime. He grabbed a bottle of Miller from the fridge and popped it open.

Did your cousin take you out to eat last night? he asked.

Yeah, Jimmy said. *I left you a note.*

His father gave a vague nod. The welding mask had left a sweaty impression in his hair, like he'd just removed a crown.

I heard there was some kind of trouble, he said. *Your cousin and his friends were mouthing off to Artie Kazmierski and his wife?*

Who told you that?

Guy I work with saw the whole thing. He said the wife was pretty upset.

Not with us, Jimmy said. *She was mad at Kaz. We were just sitting there, minding our own business, and he came over and started ragging on Wayne. He called him Jane Fonda and made fun of his flat feet.*

Jane Fonda? Jimmy's father laughed in spite of himself. *For real?*

His wife was really embarrassed. She apologized because he was being such a jerk.

Artie's a hothead, Jimmy's father conceded. *He's been that way ever since his brother died. He never got over it.*

Jimmy had been hearing that phrase his whole life—*so-and-so never got over this or that*—but he hadn't really thought about it before. It had always seemed like a figure of speech, an everyday exaggeration, like someone died laughing or froze their ass off. It hadn't occurred to him that it might be describing something real, a tragedy you couldn't recover from, a bad situation that didn't improve with time.

That whole family, his father said. *They were never the same after that.*

He'd forgotten about the beer in his hand, but then he remembered. He took a long swig, downing half the bottle in a single gulp. Then he sat down at the kitchen table and blew a weary raspberry, like the long day had finally caught up with him.

You wanna order a pizza or something? he asked.

That's okay, Jimmy told him. *I'm heading over to Greg's for a little while. We'll probably eat over there.*

He was actually going to Janie's for his sleepover with Olivia, but his father didn't need to know about that.

That's good, he said. *I'm glad you and Greg are hanging out again. I thought maybe you were going through a rough patch. You hardly ever mention his name anymore.*

We're still friends. It's just been a weird summer.

Tell me about it. His father laughed unhappily. *I guess I'll just grab a hot dog over at McCreary's. They're pretty good. They cook 'em in beer, that's the secret. Just don't get the chili on top. I learned that the hard way.*

It seemed like he was in a pretty good mood, which wasn't always the case when he got home from work, so Jimmy decided to take a chance.

Hey, Dad, he said. *Do you ever sponsor people for the union?*

The question caught his father by surprise. It wasn't the kind of thing he and Jimmy usually talked about.

Once or twice, he said. *Why?*

Hector wants to be an apprentice. He was wondering if you could help him out.

Hector? The kid next door?

Yeah. Nilda's cousin.

Jimmy's father glanced at the stove, almost like his mother was standing there, and he wanted to know her opinion. It was just a reflex, pure muscle memory. Jimmy and Denise did it all the time too.

You can't just sponsor someone out of the blue, he said. *It's for people you know. Your relatives or your neighbors . . .*

He is our neighbor. And he's kind of a relative too.

His father made a face, like that was a bridge too far.

I don't know the first thing about him, Jimmy. I don't know where he comes from. I don't even know his last name.

I'll ask him, Jimmy said. *He's a really nice guy.*

That's not the point, his father said. *I mean, what if you want to join the union someday? And then I try to sponsor you, but there's no room, because this other guy, this complete stranger, took your place. How would you feel about that?*

I don't want to join the union. So you can go ahead and give my spot to Hector.

It's not that simple, he said. *And you know it.*

And Jimmy did know it, because he'd grown up in Creamwood, and that was the kind of thing Creamwood people understood in their bones.

All right, Jimmy said. *I'll tell him you can't do it.*

His father consulted with the stove again. Then he sighed and combed his fingers through his hair, making it stick up in the front.

Tell you what, he said. *Let me talk to my shop steward and see if it's even possible.*

Really? That would be great.

His father puffed some air through his lips, like it didn't sound so great to him.

If I were you, he said, *I wouldn't get my hopes up.*

- 2 -

Jimmy was just about to leave when his father came downstairs, fresh from the shower, in shorty pajamas and a white undershirt. He stopped on the bottom of the landing.

Changed my mind, he said, in response to Jimmy's unspoken question. *Just gonna make a sandwich and watch the Yankees. Too bad you can't stick around. It's been a while since we watched a game together.*

Some other time, Jimmy told him. *I should probably get going.*

Kind of a late start. What time you coming home?

Not sure. I might sleep over. Jimmy patted his back pocket. *I'm bringing my toothbrush, just in case.*

His father nodded, like that was a good idea.

While you're at it, he said, *you might want to bring some clean underwear.*

For the rest of his life, every time he packed for an overnight trip, Jimmy would think of that moment. The sound of his father's voice, the wry look on his face, the way he stood on the stairs in those shorty pajamas. They had little red sailboats on them, and the bottoms hung all the way down to his knees.

Have fun, he said. *I'll leave the light on just in case.*

Thanks, Jimmy said. *Enjoy the game.*

There was a small diamond-shaped window cut into the front door, and some instinct made him peer through the glass before he went outside. It was a good thing too, because the Vega was parked right in front of his house with the headlights off, almost like it was on a stakeout. He could see Leonard's shadowy form in the passenger seat, his paper hat glowing faintly in the dark.

You know what? he said to his father. *I'm gonna go out the back door. I think I dropped something in the shed.*

They didn't hug goodbye, because they only ever hugged on special occasions, and this was just a regular Saturday night. Jimmy nodded and his father nodded back, and that was that.

- 3 -

He took an improvised back route to Janie's house, cutting through yards, jumping fences, slipping between garages, doing everything he could to stay off the sidewalks and stick to the shadows. It was a shortcut, but he wasn't doing it to save time. He just wanted to get where he needed to go without having to talk to Eddie or Leonard, or get anywhere near the Vega.

It wasn't easy, wending his way through the residential streets, all those little houses packed so close together. A lot of people were out on their stoops and patios, enjoying the late summer evening, or splashing around in their above-ground pools. There were surly dogs on patrol and rusty chain-link fences with jagged barbs on top. A little kid was swaying on a creaky backyard swing set, all by himself in the dark.

I seeee you, he sang out. Jimmy shushed him, like they were playing a secret game, and jogged across the lawn and out of sight.

He was sweating pretty hard by the time he got to Magnolia Road—it wasn't clean sweat, either; it was the clammy kind that smelled like fear—and he paused across the street from Janie's house to catch his breath, fix his clothes and hair, and get himself in the right frame of mind for his date with Olivia. He was just about to step out of the shadows when he heard the familiar engine growl and hurled himself to the ground a second before the Vega crawled past, pale and stealthy, its headlights extinguished. He caught a quick glimpse of Leonard—he was leaning out of the passenger window—and an even quicker one of Eddie, stone-faced behind the wheel. He couldn't see the thing in the back, but he could sense its presence, feel it scouring the darkness like a searchlight.

As soon as the car was out of sight, he hurried across the street, darted up Janie's driveway, and slipped into her house through the sliding patio doors. He thought Olivia would be waiting upstairs like the last time, but she was right there on the rec room sofa, and he didn't have time to compose himself.

Jimmy, she said, *what's the matter?*

Nothing. He tried to sound casual, but he was breathing in raggedy gulps. *You look . . . really nice.*

He meant it too. She was wearing a gauzy white dress that didn't have sleeves or straps; her bare shoulders and the top of her chest were generously coated with freckles, almost like someone had sprayed them on with a can.

Why is there dirt on your face? she asked.

Jimmy shrugged, as if to say that he often had dirt on his face for all kinds of reasons, and then he turned his attention to the coffee table. She'd arranged it with care—a fanned-out semicircle of Triscuits and an orange-and-white cheeseball on a tray, along with a bottle of Blue Nun and two wineglasses—and he felt a little embarrassed, because it looked like she'd been expecting a grown man instead of a sweaty and frightened boy.

That's a cool bottle, he said.

She stood up, licked her index and middle fingers, and wiped at the dirt on his cheek. It was a brisk maternal gesture, so familiar and unexpected that he released an involuntary whimper.

Did that hurt? she asked.

No, he said. *But I think I'm going crazy.*

He told her everything. He said that he'd seen Uncle Bob's ghost in Eddie's car—that he'd smelled it and gotten it on his skin—and that he'd just spotted the Vega a minute ago, cruising down Magnolia Road like a cop car. He said it was searching for him.

You saw Uncle Bob just now?

No, he said. *I didn't see him, but I . . . felt him . . . in my stomach . . . it's kinda hard to describe.*

She moistened her fingertips and wiped his face again, but this time it was gentler, more like a caress.

Do those other guys know he's in there? Eddie and the kid from McDonald's?

I don't think so. I'm pretty sure I'm the only one who can see him.

Jimmy, she said. *Why didn't you tell me?*

I just . . . I wasn't sure. I didn't think you'd believe me.

He was surprised by how hurt she looked.

Of course I believe you, she said. *We're in this together.*

As if to illustrate her point, she embraced him and brought her lips to his ear.

This is our special night, she whispered.

Jimmy had to do something, so he put his arms around her waist and leaned his head on her collarbone.

I brought my toothbrush, he whispered back.

- 4 -

Olivia wasn't much of a cook, but she did the best she could with a box of macaroni and cheese and a can of peas. They ate by candlelight in the dining room, sipping the Blue Nun and listening to *Tea for the Tillerman* on Mr. Randowski's stereo. She told him that her favorite song was "Wild World," and that she especially liked the line about how hard it was to get by *just upon a smile.*

So many people do that, she said. *They want you to think everything's fine, even when it's not.*

It's kinda like the backstabbers, Jimmy said. *They're smiling in your face, but they don't mean it.*

Maybe, she said, and he could tell she didn't get the reference. *I just think people need to be more honest about their feelings, don't you?*

He gave a vague nod of agreement. She looked so smart and serious, and he knew he should have been thrilled, sharing a romantic dinner with a girl he liked so much, but his nerves were shot. He was aware of a jittery sense of unease, like he needed to be somewhere else, but wasn't sure where that elsewhere might be.

Are you okay? she said. *You seem a little distracted.*

Jimmy looked down at his plate. He'd barely touched his food, except to make a neat division between the macaroni and the peas.

I'm scared, he said. *I don't know what he wants.*

She extended her leg under the table and pressed her toes against his ankle. The contact made him feel a little better.

It might not be anything bad, she said. *I mean, what if he has a message from your mother? That's what we asked him to do, right? To keep an eye out for her?*

Jimmy hadn't thought about that, the possibility that Uncle Bob had made contact with his mother and was acting as a go-between, but he hoped it wasn't true. He couldn't stand the thought of that thing being anywhere near his mother.

That was a mistake, he said. *We didn't know who he was or what he'd done.*

Olivia withdrew her foot.

We should find out, she said. *It might be important.*

When they were done eating, Jimmy cleared the plates and Olivia set up the Ouija board. It gave him the creeps to see it spread out on the table, but he understood the necessity. If Uncle Bob really did have a message from his mother, then he owed it to her to find out what it was. And if he didn't, then they could politely tell him to forget the whole thing, to stop trying to find her, and to please leave Jimmy alone.

Do you think he'll do that? he said. *If we ask him politely?*

I don't know, she said. *I think it's worth a try.*

When everything was ready, she turned off the kitchen lights and lifted the needle from the record. Jimmy didn't realize how welcome the music had been until it was gone. The silence that replaced it was absolute—a total vacuum.

She sat down across from him and placed her fingertips on the pointer. Jimmy did the same, but something was bothering him.

How are we supposed to do this?

Same as last time, she said. *Just think about Uncle Bob and see if he shows up.*

That's the thing, Jimmy told her. *Last time I wasn't thinking about Uncle Bob. I was thinking about my mother and Uncle Bob showed up. So I was wondering if maybe I should think about my mom again.*

Olivia took her hands off the pointer. Jimmy could see the candle flames reflected in her eyeglasses.

I'm not sure, she said. *How about if I think about Uncle Bob and you think about your mother? That could work, right? Cover all the bases.*

Jimmy said that sounded like a decent plan and they got back into position. She gave him a *here-goes-nothing* glance, and then she bowed her head, as if preparing to say grace. Jimmy was about to do the same when she suddenly looked up.

Wait, she said. *I almost forgot.*

She went over to the wall and removed the cheerleading photo of Janie that had bothered him the last time. She placed it face down on the table and returned to her seat.

There, she said. *Now you can concentrate.*

- 5 -

He tried to picture his mother's face, but it kept slipping away from him. It was upsetting, because she'd only been gone for three months. It didn't seem right that someone so familiar—the most important person in his life—could fade away that quickly. What would it be like in another year? A decade? What would be left of her then?

Part of his problem was that he wasn't sure which face he was trying to remember, because she'd had so many of them. She was the pretty girl in the bathing suit, and the worried bride in the wedding photo. The tired mom standing by the stove on a hot day. The sweet one kissing the top of his head. She was the proud parent, clapping in the bleachers, the concerned one examining his report card. The sick one wasting away in the bedroom, the dead one in the lime-green dress. Every time Jimmy thought about one face, it melted into another, like she didn't want to be pinned down, fixed for eternity.

It made him wonder if he'd ever actually known her—if that was even possible—because he'd never really been able to see her as a separate person from himself, an individual he could have an opinion about. She'd been part of him and he'd been part of her, and now they were on their own. He wished it was like Mrs. Cellucci had said in her condolence card, that his mother would always be right there in his heart when he needed her, but it wasn't like that. Their connection had been severed—his heart was empty—and he could barely even remember what she looked like.

- 6 -

The pointer didn't move, but he could feel the change when it happened, almost like someone had opened a window and let in the breeze. Olivia must have felt it too, because she looked up at the exact same moment Jimmy did, and both of them turned toward the living room. It looked empty, but something—someone—had arrived. Jimmy could sense its presence, and he wasn't scared at all.

Mom? he said. *Is that you?*

The pointer slid with calm certainty to the upper right-hand corner of the board.

NO.

He tried to make eye contact with Olivia, but she didn't notice. Her mouth had fallen open, like she wanted to say something but had lost the power of speech.

Are you Uncle Bob? Jimmy asked.

NO.

Then who—?

The pointer didn't hesitate. It traced a graceful descending arc and landed on the letter *D*. After resting there a second, it continued to *A*, and then drifted back to *D*.

No way, Jimmy said, because that was impossible. His father was alive and well and watching the Yankees. *You're lying.*

He tried again to get Olivia's attention, but she'd forgotten all about him. She took one hand off the pointer and brought it to her face.

Oh, Daddy, she murmured through her splayed fingers. Her voice was soft and full of wonder. *Is that really you?*

YES.

Oh my God, Olivia said. *I can't believe it.*

She sat up straight and repositioned her hands on the pointer. She gave Jimmy a wide-eyed look of amazement, and then she took a moment to pull herself together. When she finally spoke, her voice was weirdly normal, almost like she was talking on the phone.

Daddy, she said. *How are you? Are you still doing okay?*

YES.

That's good, she said. *I miss you so much. Did you miss me?*

YES.

I'm doing well, she told him. *I graduated in June. I was the valedictorian, can you believe that? I gave a speech and everything. You would have been so proud of me.*

I . . . A . . . M . . .

Olivia got a little choked up. She scrunched her face like something hurt, but then it relaxed.

I'm going to college in two weeks, Daddy. I got a full scholarship to Drew. I want to go but I'm really scared. What if I'm not ready?

The pointer wandered through the alphabet.

U . . . R . . . B . . . E . . . S . . . T . . .

She smiled and shook her head.

Of course you would say that, she told him. *I think you're the best too. I'm a little worried about Mom, though. Do you think she'll be okay without me?*

YES.

I hope so, Olivia said. *She's a hard person to live with. I mean, you should know, right? But maybe she was different back then. I can't really remember. Were you guys happy together?*

They waited for an answer, but the pointer didn't move.

Daddy? she said. *Can you hear me? Are you there?*

Jimmy could feel another change in the air—a sudden stillness—and he could tell that she felt it too.

Daddy? Her voice was softer than before, and it sounded a little desperate. *Please don't go. I have so much to tell you . . .*

They stared down at the pointer, but it just sat there, dumb and stubborn as a rock.

- 7 -

She cried for a little while and then she calmed down. She said that the exact same thing had happened the first time she talked to her father on the Ouija board—he was there and then he was gone. It was a heartbreaking experience—finding him and then losing him all over again, not even getting a chance to say goodbye—but it was worth the pain, because they'd had a moment of connection, brief as it was, and she'd been able to feel his love and tell him a little about her life.

It's like I can breathe again, she said, and Jimmy could see it in her face; it was softer and more open, like some tension had been there before and now it was gone. *I feel twenty pounds lighter.*

He was happy for her, he really was, but he was also a little annoyed, because they hadn't even been trying to reach her dad. He'd just shown up out of nowhere and hijacked the whole session.

Jimmy's bad mood didn't last for long. They went into the living room and sat down on the couch and before long they started making out and he forgot all about the Ouija board. She let him touch her breasts again, and then she pulled down the top of her dress and let him suck on her nipples, and then she guided his hand down to her underpants, which were pink with blue strawberries on them. He touched her for a while, startled by her wetness, and then she slid her hand into his shorts and tugged a few times, and he came so quickly, with such violent lurches, that it startled both of them.

Oh my God, she said. *Did I hurt you?*

No, he said. *It was just kinda . . .*

I barely even touched you, she said.

I know. It felt good, though.

She kissed him on the cheek and carefully withdrew her hand. They both stared at the mess he'd made.

Sorry, he said. *It's kinda gross.*

She brought her hand up to her nose and gave a tentative sniff. She made a face, like she wasn't sure, and then gave another sniff a second later.

It's not that bad, she said, and then she went to the bathroom to clean up.

- 8 -

Jimmy must have drifted off on the couch, because the next thing he remembered was Olivia looming over him, whispering for him to wake up. She'd changed out of her white dress into gym shorts and a baggy gray T-shirt that read *CREAMWOOD GIRLS SOFTBALL* on the front.

What happened? he mumbled.

Nothing, she told him. *You just took a little nap.*

He sat up and got his bearings. There was a bad taste in his mouth and a damp patch on the front of his underpants.

What time is it?

A little after midnight. Why don't you brush your teeth and come to bed?

I just woke up. I don't think I can—

We don't have to go right to sleep, she said. *We could talk a little or I could read to you. Whatever you want.*

Read to me? What, like a bedtime story?

She shrugged, like there was nothing wrong with that, and then she grabbed his hand and helped him to his feet.

Let's just get under the covers, she said. *And then we'll see what happens.*

He was still only half-awake when he got to the bathroom, and not very happy with himself. It was embarrassing, nodding off like that, leaving Olivia alone for however long it had been. It made him feel like he was a little kid and she was his babysitter, and it didn't help that she was joking about reading him a bedtime story, though he wasn't completely sure it was a joke.

He peed and washed his hands and splashed some cold water on his face, and that was when he saw the Trojan. It was just sitting there on the flat part of the sink, right next to the Aim toothpaste and a bottle of Listerine, almost like Mr. Randowski had left it there when he went down the shore, except that Jimmy had been in the same bathroom earlier in the evening, and there hadn't been any Trojans on the sink top. He picked it up and read the words on the front.

One rolled latex condom.

The envelope was powder blue, almost but not quite the same shade as the Vega, and the object inside was designed *For Those Who Wish a Special End as a Receptacle,* whatever that meant. It wasn't the first time Jimmy had seen one—Eddie had shown him the crinkled Ramses he'd been carrying in his wallet for what appeared to be a very long time—but he had no idea what an actual rubber would look like if he took it out of the package, or how he might go about putting it on. That wasn't the kind of thing they'd covered in eighth-grade health class.

He slipped it into his pocket, and then he dried his face and squeezed some striped toothpaste onto his brush. He ran it under the faucet and brought it up to his mouth.

Honey, his mother said, and it was like she was standing right next to him. *It's time to go home.*

It was such an amazing feeling, to hear her voice again after all that time, to know that she was nearby and hadn't abandoned him. It was so much better than a Ouija board.

The only problem was, he didn't want to leave just then, not with a Trojan in his pocket and Olivia waiting in the bedroom. His mind wasn't a hundred percent sure it was ready for what she wanted him to do—some part of him was terrified—but his body was more than willing to give it a try.

It's a sleepover, he told her, though the words were only in his head. *I'll go home in the morning.*

You shouldn't be here, she said. *You're too young for this.*

He wanted to tell her that he wasn't a kid anymore, that he'd grown up over the course of the summer, but he knew she wouldn't believe him, and he wasn't even sure if it was true.

James Francis Perrini, she said, in a voice you weren't allowed to argue with. *You need to go home right now.*

He felt like a coward, tiptoeing down to the rec room, exiting through the sliding glass doors without saying goodbye, but there was no way he could face Olivia like that, not with his mother standing at his side.

- 9 -

Her presence had been strong inside the house, but it faded when he stepped outside. He felt cheated, like she'd called him on the phone and then hung up before they could start a conversation. It was a lot like the night of her wake, when she'd told him it was okay to leave the funeral home, but not where to go after that.

It occurred to him that maybe this was all he was ever going to get from her, these brief visitations when she interrupted his life to dispense a completely ordinary piece of advice—something he already knew because she'd already told him—a memory in the form of a ghost.

Get some fresh air.

Save the sex for when you're older.

It was better than nothing, because at least he got to hear her voice again, but it cost him something too—this feeling of renewed loss, a sense of being abandoned all over again, not that it was her fault. None of it was her fault. If she'd had a choice, she never would have left him in the first place, and he wouldn't have been out here right now, feeling sorry for himself at one o'clock in the morning.

He was alone on the sidewalk, absorbed in his thoughts, and he yelped out loud when the Vega came squealing around the corner of Sycamore Street, blinding him in the glare of its headlights. He was even more shocked when it barreled right past him, as if they didn't even see him, as if he was beneath their notice, as inconsequential as a tree trunk or a stop sign.

- 10 -

There must have been sirens at some earlier point in the night, but Jimmy hadn't heard them. And there must have been a burning smell in the air, but he'd missed that too. He had no idea of what he was coming home to until he turned onto Morgan Street and saw the flashing lights and the emergency vehicles, and that was when he started to run, because it was all happening right in front of his house. But then he got closer and realized, with a feeling of relief that also filled him with shame, that it wasn't his house after all.

It was Wayne and Nilda's.

He'd never seen a fire like that before, so angry and out of control, snarling and popping and hissing, greasy black smoke billowing from the broken windows, spark fountains blasting through the roof and into the sky. Firemen were running around in their heavy coats and helmets, spraying huge arcing jets of water that didn't seem to have any effect at all, and two of them were standing on the front stoop, shouting into the cavity where the door had been—one of them had smashed it open with an ax—asking if anyone was in there, if anyone could hear them.

A small crowd of spectators had gathered across the street, some in their pajamas and bathrobes, their faces reddened by the glow of the flames. Jimmy couldn't spot Wayne or Nilda or Hector or Yvette among the onlookers, and he wondered if they might be out somewhere having a good time, maybe dancing at a party, and didn't even know what was going on. Or maybe—it was a huge relief when it occurred to him—maybe they were hunkered down in his own house, sitting safe and sound around the kitchen table, because Jimmy's house was fine, utterly untouched by the flames.

It looked the way it always did, small and tidy and unassuming, as familiar as his own face in the mirror. The downstairs lights were on, and the TV was flickering in the living room. Maybe his father was in there too, because Jimmy hadn't been able to spot him among the volunteer firemen, which didn't make a lot of sense, since he would have had to be the first one on the scene.

He walked up the front steps and went inside—no one tried to stop him—but the living room was empty, and so was the kitchen. He called his father's name and then his sister's name, even though Denise was out of town, and then he tried Wayne's and Nilda's and Hector's, and got the same silence in return. Just to be sure, he went upstairs and checked all the rooms, but everything was perfectly still, like some kind of museum exhibit, *The House Where the Perrinis Used to Live.*

Jimmy's bedroom window looked straight across the driveway to the inferno next door. When he pressed his face against the glass, he could feel the heat from the flames, and he could see the ladder leaning against the outside wall of Wayne and Nilda's house, stretching up to a window on the second floor. It was his father's extension ladder, the one he used to clean the gutters, and the window it led to wasn't really a window anymore, just a charred orifice where the smoke poured out.

- 11 -

He went back outside and walked up to the first fireman he saw. It turned out to be Mr. Cellucci, though it took a moment to recognize him in his uniform, his face shadowed by the brim of his helmet.

Excuse me, he said. *Have you seen my father?*

Mr. Cellucci looked bewildered, like Jimmy's question made no sense.

Oh, Jesus, he said, and his voice was all wrong. *Jimmy. Son. You shouldn't be here.*

Jimmy pointed at the house. *Is he in there?*

I don't know, Mr. Cellucci said, but it sounded like he did. *There's too much smoke. We can't—*

Another fireman came rushing over, an older guy with a white mustache. His name was Kenny, and he played first base on the fire department softball team. He glared at Mr. Cellucci.

Goddammit, Richie. Get him outta here.

What should I do with him? Mr. Cellucci asked.

I don't know, Kenny said. *Find one of the neighbors or something. Just get him the hell away from here.*

Mr. Cellucci turned to Jimmy with a pleading look on his face.

Is there anywhere you can go for a little while?

I can't leave, Jimmy said. *Not until I talk to him.*

There was a brief standoff, the three of them standing there, staring at one another, until a cop appeared at Jimmy's side. He was a youngish guy, not very tall, but with a weightlifter's chest and shoulders.

You're Jimmy, right?

Yeah, Jimmy said. *I'm trying to find my father.*

The cop nodded, like that was a perfectly reasonable goal to have.

Everyone's doing their best, he said, and somehow they were already on the move, the cop's hand on the small of Jimmy's back, propelling him down the driveway and across the street to a patrol car parked in front of the Jusczkas' house. *I need you to do me a favor, Jimmy.*

What kind of favor? Jimmy asked.

The cop opened the door and guided Jimmy into the back seat, almost like he was placing him under arrest.

Just sit tight, he said. *I'll be back in a minute.*

And then the door slammed and the cop walked away.

- 12 -

Jimmy didn't trust his memory of what happened after that, because it couldn't possibly have unfolded the way he remembered.

The broad strokes must have been correct. He was trapped in the back of the police car and the house kept burning and more and more people kept showing up to watch. That part wasn't so unusual—crowds always gathered at the sites of fires or accidents—except that it was really late at night, and some of the spectators he remembered seeing were little kids, and some of them were old people with canes and walkers. There were young couples holding hands and groups of teenagers chatting among themselves. There was an older woman in a bathing suit, with a towel wrapped around her waist, like she'd wandered over from a midnight swim.

It started to feel like a block party, like the whole town was there, including lots of Jimmy's friends and acquaintances. Some of the counselors from Rec in their yellow shirts, a few Mosquito Control teammates in their red hats. Father Paul in his short-sleeved black shirt with the white collar, and Mr. Kazmierski and his pregnant wife, all dressed up, like they'd just come back from a wedding.

It was more like a nightmare than a memory, the real and the imagined all jumbled together. Mr. and Mrs. Felice in their lawn chairs, as if they'd hopped in the car and driven all the way from Pennsylvania to join the festivities. The whole Randowski family, even though they were down the shore. He could've sworn that Denise was there too, even though she was sleeping in a tent on the bank of the Delaware River. She wasn't smiling or anything, but she didn't seem especially upset. She was just standing there, watching the fire with everyone else.

The blaze was more or less under control by the time Eddie and Leonard showed up. They arrived together, making their way down the sidewalk from the direction of Main Street, but then they separated, Eddie veering toward the front of the crowd and Leonard drifting into the back, removing his paper cap as he melted in with the onlookers.

A team of firemen had already entered the house by the time Olivia got there. She floated right past Jimmy, barefoot in her gauzy white dress. He called her name and pounded on the window, but she didn't hear him, didn't even glance in his direction. She just wandered into the throng of bodies and disappeared from view.

And then something wonderful happened.

It started as a commotion in the crowd, bodies swaying and jostling, and then the spectators parted like the Red Sea, and Wayne and Nilda stumbled into view. Jimmy had assumed that they were trapped inside the burning house, and the sight of them made him gasp in amazement, as if they'd returned from the dead.

He waited breathlessly for the others to appear—for the miracle to complete itself—but the crowd had already sealed itself up like a wound. It was just Wayne and Nilda standing in the street, holding hands, staring at the smoldering ruins of their home.

An older cop approached them with a wary expression. Nilda pointed at the house and asked a question, and the cop shook his head no. Wayne asked something else and got the same answer, and then Nilda's knees buckled and she clapped her hand to her mouth. Wayne tried to comfort her, but she jerked away from him and turned to face the crowd. She hesitated for a moment or two, like she wanted to say something, maybe even make a speech, and then she threw her head back and released a howl of agony, a sound so awful that Jimmy had to close his eyes and cover his ears, and that was the last thing he remembered.

I told myself I was going back for my family's sake—to support my sister and honor my father's memory—but it wasn't just that.

I was doing it for myself.

I was tired of denying the past. My entire childhood like a phantom limb, a dull ache where the missing part used to be. It felt like I was finally ready to face up to it, to reclaim those missing years, the world I'd left behind.

That's the dream, right? To look at yourself and be at peace with the person you were and the person you've become. The things you were stuck with and the things you got to choose. You can't just erase the parts you don't like or hide from the ones that scare you or make you feel ashamed.

I wanted to be whole again.

That was why I went back to Creamwood.

I arrived in Newark on a Friday afternoon in mid-September. I was on my own. Molly had hoped to join me, but her father was moving into assisted living and needed some help with the transition, so she'd changed her plans at the last minute.

My sister had to work—she was the office manager for a dental practice in North Drumford—but I was met at the airport by Mayor Rodriguez-Manzoni, who had kindly offered to take me on a tour of my old haunts before my appearance at the library. She was an upbeat woman in her midforties, a Realtor and mother of two, big sunglasses and pointy turquoise fingernails that she liked to drum on the steering wheel of her Lexus.

"It's very kind of you," I said, "but I could've taken a cab."

"Don't be silly," she said. "You're the guest of honor. I'm just sorry we couldn't cover the airfare."

"No worries," I said. "It's a write-off. You know, with the book signing and everything. I can deduct the travel expenses."

"Oh." Without checking her mirrors, she sliced across two lanes of traffic to take a left-hand exit. "I wasn't aware of that. Good for *you.*"

We were silent for a minute or two as the GPS guided her through the roads outside the airport, which were a lot more convoluted than I remembered.

"Everyone's really excited about your visit," she told me, once we'd found our way onto Route 22. "We're expecting a capacity crowd."

In my memory, Creamwood was a dark and daunting place, full of grief and ghosts, funeral flowers, and the stench of something burning. In broad daylight, though, it just looked like a friendly little town, a nice place to raise your kids. Wide streets, affordable homes, healthy lawns, and shady trees.

Nothing to be scared of.

A lot had changed in fifty years. Most of the factories that used to line the railroad tracks were gone, replaced by luxury apartment buildings and mini-malls and a surprising number of restaurants. On Grand Avenue alone, you could dine at an Indian place, a vegan noodle café, a Tex-Mex cantina, and a Brazilian barbecue grill, and that's just a partial list.

"We've become a dining destination," the mayor told me. "*New Jersey Monthly* just did a big roundup, *'Top Ten Foodie Outposts in the Burbs,'* something like that. We were number four. And that's the whole state, not just Union County."

"Wow," I said. "It was just burgers and pizza when I was a kid. And a couple of Chinese places."

"We're a lot more diverse these days," she said. "We're really proud of that."

It wasn't just the food, of course. The people of Creamwood were different too. I saw an Asian grandfather pushing a baby carriage down the sidewalk, and a woman in an orange sari checking her mailbox. I shouldn't have been shocked to see a young Black father carrying his little daughter out of a house on Fox Hollow Road, but I was, just for a second—the same way I'd been surprised to see Hector sitting on my front stoop all those years ago—and then I felt a sense of lightness and relief, like a flaw had been repaired in my absence, a crooked thing made straight.

The mayor must have noticed my double take.

"It's not like it used to be," she told me. "Everyone's welcome now."

"When did it change?" I asked.

"Late eighties," she said. "Maybe early nineties. Before my time."

"Was there any trouble?"

"Nothing too serious," she said. "Some of the senior citizens are still a little grumpy about it."

I asked to see my old elementary school—a forbidding brick fortress with tiny windows that looked like gun turrets—but it had been demolished a long time ago. The new building was a lot more cheerful, a rambling low-slung structure with colorful siding and lots of tinted glass, a soccer field and a rubber-carpeted playground in the back.

"When I was a kid the whole schoolyard was paved," I said. "We had a set of rusty monkey bars, but that was about it. If you fell, you were outta luck." I heard myself and laughed. "I sound like Grampa Simpson."

"I know all about the bad old days," the mayor told me. "My next-door neighbor grew up here. Heather Horak? I think her last name was Cataldo back then. She says she knew you."

"Heather, wow. We were summer recreation counselors back in the day. She wore tube tops and smoked in front of the kids. You could get away with that back then."

"No more tube tops for Heather," the mayor told me. "But she still smokes like a fiend. I can't even go inside her house. It smells like an ashtray."

"That was how the whole world used to smell," I said. "Nobody even noticed."

The old high school was still there—the mayor said it was in terrible shape—but it wasn't exactly the same. The sports teams had been the Chiefs when I was a kid, but there must have been some objections, because the LED marquee out front flashed the motto *THIS IS CARDINALS' COUNTRY* over and over, interspersed with optimistic declarations like *CREAMWOOD COMPOSTS and EXCELLENCE IS ORDINARY HERE.*

We stopped at a red light by the practice fields, and I gazed through the window at the football players and soccer players and field hockey players, and something about the spectacle of all those healthy teenagers running around and calling out to one another under the bright blue sky made me feel a pang of sadness for the boy I'd been.

"Do you want to go inside?" the mayor asked. "I could take a picture of you in front of your old locker if you want. We could post it on the town Instagram. We're trying to be a little more active on social media."

"I don't have an old locker," I told her. "I never actually made it to the high school. I left a week before my freshman year was supposed to start. You know, right after the fire."

The mayor made a soft humming sound.

"I'm sorry for your loss," she said. "That must have been so hard for you."

"Must have been," I said. "I can't really remember."

I wasn't lying about that. There's a hole in my timeline that starts on the night of the fire and lasts for a couple of months. I have no recollection of attending my father's funeral—I'm sure I did, I must have—and none of Hector's, either, though I'm guessing I didn't go to his. They were the only two casualties. (I'm not sure where Yvette was that night, but she wasn't in the house with Hector, and I never saw her again.)

I don't remember packing my stuff or moving to Barrington Heights or any discussion about what school I would attend, and I don't remember saying goodbye to any of my Creamwood friends, the few I had left. When my memory starts up again, it's late fall and I'm a freshman at Christian Brothers Prep, a shell-shocked kid named Jamie wearing a ridiculous uniform—white shirt and a clip-on tie—and there's not a girl in sight. I took the bus home to my Uncle Al and Aunt Gina's gigantic house, which had a circular driveway and the heated pool that my father had loved to hate. Wayne and Nilda were living there too, but Nilda was unhappy—she and Aunt Gina couldn't stand each other—and she moved out in the spring. (Denise had opted not to join us; she'd gotten back together with Nick, and had followed him to Delaware. She said she wanted to enroll in the university, maybe study nursing, but it never happened. She got pregnant in the spring, and they moved back home to be closer to Nick's family.)

The following year—right around the time my Uncle Al got arrested in a bribery and kickback scandal (my father had been right about that)—I got sent to boarding school at Branchbrook Academy, where I learned to play tennis and golf and dress like a preppie. I wrote poetry and edited the literary magazine and did well enough to get admitted to Princeton, where I majored in creative writing. Molly was in my class, but I didn't meet her until after we graduated. We fell in love, spent our midtwenties in Park Slope, and then we moved to Iowa City and then to Chicago and finally to Los Angeles. We raised our kids and I wrote my books and screenplays, and I did my best to forget about Creamwood and the life there that I never got to live.

I barely recognized our old house on Morgan Street. The changes were mostly cosmetic—the exterior painted blue instead of gray, some new shrubs and landscaping flourishes—but it seemed even smaller than I remembered, and a little shabbier, mainly because many of the surrounding homes had been renovated or knocked down and replaced in the intervening years. The whole neighborhood had gotten an upgrade—it felt brighter, more prosperous, a little more aspirational than it had been during my childhood.

"Do you want to go inside?" the mayor asked. "I know the family who lives here now. I'm sure they'd be happy to let you have a look around."

The adult in me—the writer—wanted to say, Yes, of course I want to see the inside of my childhood home, but the kid in me couldn't do it. Whatever it was I'd find in there—a treasure trove of lost memories or a place I no longer recognized—I knew it would break my heart. It was hard enough just standing out on the sidewalk.

"That's okay," I said. "I don't want to bother anyone."

"They're lovely people," she assured me. "The wife's a Vietnamese refugee. Came over on the boats when she was little. The husband does something with solar panels."

I stared at the front door—it was a new one, no more diamond-shaped window—and tried to remember what it was like to live in that house before my mother got sick, back when it was the only home I'd ever known. I'd felt safe in there, watched over, doted on, and I'd taken those feelings with me when I went outside. I wasn't scared of anything.

"Remind me," the mayor said. "Which house was it that burned down?"

I pointed at the boxy white colonial that had replaced Wayne and Nilda's house.

"Such a shame," she muttered. "I heard someone fell asleep with a lit cigarette. I guess that happened a lot in those days."

"I never heard anything about a cigarette," I told her. "I heard it was a candle that tipped over."

"Huh," she said. "Maybe I got the details wrong."

I wasn't all that clear about it myself. Nobody had talked much about the fire after it happened, at least not in my presence. All I knew was that the authorities had done an investigation, and that was the conclusion they came up with. There was an article about it in the *Star-Ledger.*

"Candle Started Fatal Creamwood Blaze."

I never really believed it, though. I couldn't picture it in my mind, Hector all alone in the house, lighting a candle and setting it down on an uneven surface, somewhere it could easily tip over. A smoldering cigarette or joint seemed a little more plausible, but I didn't believe that, either.

"I don't think it was an accident," I said.

The mayor turned and looked at me, her eyes concealed behind her sunglasses.

"Excuse me?"

"I think it might have been arson. You know, because of Hector? The other person who died that night. He was a houseguest of my cousin and his wife and . . . he was Black . . . and I think some people didn't like it that he was living there. I'm not sure if they meant to kill anyone. I think they were probably just trying to send a message."

The mayor removed her sunglasses. She didn't look happy.

"That's a serious accusation," she said. "Do you have any proof?"

"No," I said. "But it's the only explanation that makes any sense to me."

She put her sunglasses back on and gave me a tight smile.

"I really hope you're wrong about that," she said. "We're all just trying to live together now, you know?"

I didn't argue with her. I really hoped I was wrong too.

"His name was Hector Lopez," I told her. I hadn't known that until I read it in the newspaper. "He was a nice guy. He wanted to be a welder. You should name a building after him too."

* * *

The library was located inside the new municipal building, which took up half a block of Main Street, and also housed the police station, the fire department, and various offices of the town government. Even though it was the explicit reason for my visit, I was still startled and unexpectedly moved to see my father's name emblazoned over the main entrance in raised black letters: *THE FRANK J. PERRINI MEMORIAL COMPLEX.*

There was a heroic oil painting of my dad in the lobby, the first thing you saw when you went inside. The artist had depicted him in full firefighter regalia—the black raincoat and matching pants, both with reflective yellow stripes, and the hard red helmet that I loved to wear around the house as a kid, even though it was heavier than it looked and always slipped down over my eyes. In the painting, he's standing in front of a fire truck, aiming a hose at the viewer, his face younger and more handsome than it had been at the time of his death, his eyes full of a steely determination that made him look like a stranger to me, a movie star playing the role of my father. There was a plaque beneath the painting, explaining that Frank J. Perrini had lost his life on the night of August 24, 1974, in a brave attempt to rescue a neighbor from a house fire, the only Creamwood first responder ever to lose his life in the line of duty.

We honor your sacrifice, it concluded. *You have our enduring gratitude. Semper Fi.*

I wondered what my father would have made of it. He didn't have much of an ego, and had never liked to call attention to himself. He probably would have taken issue with the *Semper Fi,* because he hadn't been a marine, just a cargo loader in the Air Force. But the rest was true. He'd climbed that ladder in his sailboat pajamas and disappeared into a burning house. I'm not sure where he found the courage to do that, but he did it, and I'm guessing that he didn't even hesitate, that it never even occurred to him that there might be another course of action available to him. He was a fireman, and there was a fire, and I'm sure he was terrified, but the fear and the heat and flames didn't stop him from stepping onto that ladder, reaching up for the next rung and the rung after that.

He was just forty at the time of his death, more than twenty years younger than I was that September evening, but I felt like a little boy standing in front of his portrait, and I missed him in a way I hadn't for a very long time.

A middle-aged woman was waiting near the entrance of the library, right next to a poster advertising my event. Her face lit up when she saw me.

"Jay Perry," she said, stepping forward and grasping my hand in both of hers. She had graying hair and a youthful face and a fondness for chunky jewelry. "It's an honor to meet you. Welcome back to Creamwood."

"Thanks," I said. "Nice to meet you too."

"I'm Cathleen," she said. "Cathleen Kazmierski."

"Cathy's our superstar librarian," the mayor told me. "She just took over last year and she's been a real breath of fresh air."

"Kazmierski?" I said. "Are you—?"

She nodded, a little sheepishly.

"Arthur was my dad," she said. "You were one of his students, right?"

"Long time ago. How's he doing?"

"He's gone," she said. "Passed away a couple of years ago. Covid. It was awful."

"I'm sorry to hear that."

"Tragic," the mayor added. "He was such a popular teacher."

"It was his own fault," Cathleen told me. "He wouldn't get the vaccine, wouldn't wear a mask, wouldn't go to the hospital when he got sick. He thought it was all a big hoax. It was really tough on my mom."

"Is she . . . okay?" I asked.

"She's fine," Cathleen said. "A few health issues, but nothing she can't manage. Did you know her?"

"Not well. I met her once or twice before I moved away. She was pregnant with her first child. I don't know if that was you or—"

"That was definitely me," she said. "I'm the one and only heir to the Kazmierski fortune."

"Amazing," the mayor said. "Such a small world."

"Well," I said, "it's nice to meet the finished product. Please give my regards to your mom."

"I will. She was hoping to come tonight, but she's a little under the weather. Not Covid, though, just a regular old cold."

"Something's going around," the mayor said. "We had a lot of no-shows at the senior meeting yesterday."

Cathleen shook her head and gave me the apologetic half smile I knew all too well from my early years as a novelist and short story writer, when I'd suffered through too many poorly attended bookstore and library events to count.

"I hope it doesn't affect our turnout," she told me.

My talk was scheduled for seven o'clock, but attendance was light, so we held off for a while to accommodate the stragglers. The people trickling in were a mix of strangers and familiar faces, including my sister and Nick, who'd mercifully left their MAGA hats at home, and Greg and Janie, who were married and still living in town. Janie looked pretty good—like she might fit into her old cheerleading outfit in a pinch—but her skin was weathered and leathery, probably from all those summers on the beach before the invention of sunscreen. Greg was bulky and lumbering in a way that surprised me—he'd always been such a graceful athlete as a kid—and he stared at me with a sour expression, as if the taste of my dirty sneakers was still fresh on his lips.

It took me a few seconds to recognize Larry Brunner, who'd arrived with a woman who must have been twenty years younger than he was. He'd cut his hair and been fitted with prosthetic legs since the last time I'd seen him rolling down the street, shouting obscenities into the night. He wheeled himself over and gave me a fist bump.

"I remember you," he said. "Used to see you walking around town sometimes."

"I remember you too."

"I'm not that guy anymore," he told me. "I hadn't found Jesus back then and I hadn't met Mary Lou."

He glanced up at his companion, who had just wandered over to join us. She was a plump woman with tired eyes and a cautious smile.

"I'm a very lucky man," he said.

"The Lord blessed us both," she told me, and then she bent down and kissed him on the cheek.

We started the program at quarter after. There were maybe twenty-five people in the audience by then—not the smallest group I'd ever spoken to, but a disappointing turnout nonetheless. Only half of the folding chairs were occupied, the empty seats staring back at me like a reproach. I smiled politely through Cathleen's flattering introduction, but my eyes kept drifting over to the doorway, as if I were expecting someone else to arrive at any moment, someone important, though I wasn't quite sure who that someone might be.

I guess I was hoping Olivia might make an appearance, but I knew the odds were against it. I had never seen her after the fire, and never heard a word about what had become of her. I'd googled her name on several occasions, searched for her on Facebook, and even contacted the Drew University alumni office, but it was like she'd dropped off the face of the earth. Her mother had died back in the eighties, and the old Poodle Pete building where they'd lived had been torn down, replaced by the Creamwood Wellness Co-op, home to an impressive array of physical therapists, Reiki practitioners, and personal trainers.

I knew Eddie wouldn't be coming, because he'd died in a car crash in 1992. The only surprise was that it hadn't been his fault, at least according to the article I'd read. It said he'd been minding his business, driving down Route 46 in the middle of the afternoon, when a school bus drifted across the center line and hit him head-on.

I had no idea if Leonard was still around, and no way of finding out, because I'd never known his last name. Not that it mattered much. I didn't want to see him, and didn't think there was much of a chance of him darkening the door of a public library under any circumstances.

I began my presentation by giving a brief history of my literary career, doing my best to keep things breezy and self-deprecating. I talked about how poorly my "serious" books had sold, and the crisis that had led to the writing of the original version of *Ghost Teacher*—the grisly horror novel that no one wanted to publish—and then the more uplifting revision that had changed my life for better and worse.

"That's the thing about writing," I said. "It's all a big mystery. You don't know where your ideas come from, you don't know how to get them onto the page, and you have no idea how the world's going to react to them. You've got to learn to be comfortable with the not knowing, or at least learn to live with it."

Then I told them about my recent, deeply frustrating bout of writer's block, the melancholy and debilitating sense I'd had during the past few years that my creative life was over, that I had nothing left to say, and no right to stand in front of an audience and call myself a writer anymore.

"That was one of the reasons I didn't want to come here tonight," I explained. "I'm only standing in front of you right now because my sister guilted me into it."

Denise stared at me from the second row. She looked startled and a little put out.

"It's okay," I told her. "I'm glad you did. It got me thinking about the past and I don't know . . . I guess I just started remembering some things I hadn't let myself think about for a long time."

I pulled a folded wad of paper from my back pocket and flattened it out on the podium.

"This is the beginning of something new," I said. "I just started it a couple of weeks ago. I'm calling it *Ghost Town* for the time being. It's about my last summer in Creamwood."

I took a deep breath and let it out slowly. It's a vulnerable moment, reading new material out loud for the first time, exposing your baby to the world's judgment, and it's an even dicier proposition if your audience includes some of the people you've been writing about.

"If anyone asked him about his childhood," I began, *"he always gave the same answer. 'For a while there,' he would say, 'we were a normal family.' There were four of them, Mom, Dad, Denise, and Jimmy."*

My voice was shaky at first, but it got steadier as I went along. The audience was with me—I could feel it—and I started to relax a little. I was telling my story and listening to it at the same time, watching it take shape in my mind, halfway between a movie and a dream.

A boy steps out of his house on a mild spring evening, a boy in a baseball uniform. He hops on his bike and cruises through the streets of his hometown, the only place he's ever lived, a town that might as well be the whole world. There's a soft breeze, he feels lighthearted, vaguely optimistic, ready for the big game he's about to play. There's a girl he likes, and he's hoping she might be there, watching from the bleachers.

I've been told I'm a pretty good reader. I take my time, pay close attention to the rhythm of the prose, the stops and starts, the spaces between the phrases, the way one sentence flows into another. The only criticism I get is that I don't make enough eye contact with the audience, and it's a valid one. I don't like lifting my eyes from the page, losing my thread, breaking the spell of the narrative.

That was why I felt it before I saw it. It came as a sudden rush of remorse, that hopeless feeling you sometimes have upon waking from a bad dream, like you'd done something terrible to someone you loved and would never be forgiven. I looked up and it was right in front of me, that glitch in the air—Uncle Bob or whatever it was—suspended above an empty seat in the front row.

I closed my eyes and willed it away, but it was still there when I opened them, floating directly in front of me, ruining everything, and then I saw that my mother was sitting right next to it, in a chair that had been empty the moment before. She was wearing her funeral dress, and she was smiling, like she couldn't have been happier to see me, or prouder of the person I'd become.

Don't get me wrong. I'm not saying she was really there. I couldn't see her that well—her dress was a green smudge and face was blurry, like her features had been worn away by time, but I could feel her love as clearly as I could feel the rage and hatred and self-pity radiating from the shameful thing beside her. It was almost too much, those two ghosts so close together, and the audience staring back at me, wondering why I'd stopped reading in the middle of a sentence and was just standing there with what must have been a sick and stricken look on my face.

I gripped the podium with both hands to steady myself, and did the only thing I knew how to do. I averted my eyes from Uncle Bob and concentrated on my mother. I concentrated as hard as I could, until her love was the only thing I could feel, and then I found my place on the page and continued with my story.

ACKNOWLEDGMENTS

I'm fortunate to work with so many good people, whose advice and support come in so many different forms—my agent, Maria Massie, my editor Kathy Belden (and the entire team at Scribner), Sylvie Rabineau, Albert Berger, and Ron Yerxa, among many others. I'm grateful to my family as well—to Mary, Nina, and Luke, and also to my brother and sister. Our mom died while I was writing this book, and her absence has only made me realize more clearly than ever how lucky we were to have her in our lives.

ABOUT THE AUTHOR

Tom Perrotta is the bestselling author of eleven works of fiction, including *Election* and *Little Children*, both of which were made into critically acclaimed movies, and *The Leftovers* and *Mrs. Fletcher*, which were both adapted into HBO series. He lives outside Boston.